I0525223

IN A FLASH

ALSO BY KERRY KEENE

The Proudest Yankees of All
Tales from the Boston Bruins Locker Room
1951
Fenway Park
Relentless Pursuit
Number 4 Bobby Orr
Dodgers in the Hall of Fame
Red Sox in the Hall of Fame
Yankees in the Hall of Fame
The Other Me

IN A FLASH

a novel

KERRY KEENE

In a Flash
Copyright © 2025 Kerry Keene

Produced and printed by Stillwater River Publications.
All rights reserved. Written and produced in the United
States of America. This book may not be reproduced
or sold in any form without the expressed, written
permission of the author(s) and publisher.

Visit our website at
www.StillwaterPress.com
for more information.

First Stillwater River Publications Edition.

ISBN: 978-1-968548-02-5

1 2 3 4 5 6 7 8 9 10
Cover design by Elisha Gillette.
Interior book design by Matthew St. Jean.
Published by Stillwater River Publications,
West Warwick, RI, USA.

*The views and opinions expressed in this book are solely
those of the author(s) and do not necessarily reflect
the views and opinions of the publisher.*

IN A FLASH

1

HE WOULD LOOK back on this day countless times over the course of his life, but at this moment, it was his final class of the day on a Friday afternoon, and Christian Casey could only focus on the clock. All he was looking forward to was his high school golf team's match against a rival Rhode Island school that would begin in one hour. He had three weeks left to go in his senior year at Portsmouth High School, and he could finally put classrooms behind him. Though he had always been a good student, he did not see where college would play a role in his future. Christian had three main pursuits in mind for the years ahead. He was being groomed to play an important role at his father's very high-end foreign auto dealership in Newport; he wanted to pursue a career in professional golf; and he wanted to play the cello in the Providence Symphony Orchestra. He had developed an unusual passion for the instrument as a young boy and had practiced almost religiously since. He was in almost no way a typical eighteen-year-old boy.

As he often did, he got to drive expensive used vehicles from his father's dealership, and this day's choice was a 2005 Bentley sedan. Christian and two fellow members of the golf team arrived at the course twenty minutes before the start of the match.

As the boys gathered near the area where they would tee off, everyone noticed that the sky had grown very dark quickly. The coaches of the two teams got together to confer as to whether they should call it off. At that moment, set to be the first to tee off, Christian began taking practice swings. On his third swing, there was a tremendous crack of thunder and a brilliant flash of lightning that lit up the sky for nearly five seconds. In the middle of a swing with his golf club pointed skyward, Christian was struck by a bolt and dropped to the ground as if he were shot.

The student golfers immediately ran for the safety of the clubhouse. The two coaches seemed uncertain of what to do, looking back and forth at each other. One asked the other "Is it safe to touch him?"

As Christian appeared completely lifeless, his coach pulled out his phone and called for an ambulance. He then reached down and placed two fingers on the boy's neck and found that there was a weak pulse and said to the other "Well... somehow... he's still alive."

The ambulance arrived a few moments later and he was strapped on to a stretcher and then driven off to Newport Hospital. Golf coach Higgins notified the high school, who immediately called his mother Emily Casey. She arrived at the hospital emergency room shortly after he had been brought in, and before she was allowed to see him. She was approached by a doctor who had a very grim look on his face. Expecting the worst, she let out a scream and nearly dropped to her knees.

"Mrs. Casey" he quickly stated. "He is alive and breathing, but unfortunately at this time he is completely unresponsive. We're going to begin doing several tests, but for the time being, we simply do not have any solid answers."

"Can I see him?' she asked.

"Just for a couple of minutes" the doctor replied. "We have to start doing tests very soon."

She was then led by a nurse to the room where her son was lying completely motionless on a gurney. Seeing him, she began sobbing uncontrollably and hollered "How could those bastards let him be on a golf course in a thunderstorm?'

At that moment, her husband Bryan entered the room and Emily collapsed in his arms. Their sixteen-year-old daughter Shannon entered the room just behind him and walked slowly over to where he lay. She turned to her mother and said "Mum... I was afraid he'd be all burned... but he doesn't seem to have a mark on him."

Her father responded, "It's what's going on inside that we have no idea about."

At that moment a doctor came over to the family and introduced himself and said "Mr. and Mrs. Casey, we're going to do everything we can, but we won't know much until we do several tests. Right now, we have to do a CT scan and various other procedures. We'll keep you informed."

With that, Emily walked over and gave Christian a kiss on the forehead, and her tears dripped onto his face. She whispered in his ear, "We won't leave you honey .... please don't leave us."

They all had tears in their eyes as the hospital personnel began to wheel him through a large set of swinging doors. It was just the beginning of a long, harrowing time for the Casey family.

2

AFTER THE COMPLETION of several tests performed on Christian, doctors drew no solid conclusions and essentially determined him to be in a comatose state. He was admitted to the hospital's Intensive care unit where he could be monitored closely. Visitors were only allowed in that unit for brief periods at a time, and his mother decided she would stay the night and sleep in a nearby waiting room. She got special permission from the nurse in charge to be able to peek in on him every couple of hours for a minute or two.

The following day, dozens of family members and friends came to visit. It was decided among the immediate family that they would keep a constant vigil as close to Christian as the hospital would allow. They would basically rotate between Emily, father Bryan, sister Shannon, and Aunt Jesse, Emily's sister.

Late Saturday evening, with his father Bryan sitting in the waiting room, a nurse came out and said to him, "Mr. Casey, I think you better come in. Things are not looking good." She escorted him to Christian's bed and said "His blood pressure has dropped dangerously low, and his heartbeat is very weak. I think maybe you better call your wife."

When Emily and Shannon walked into the Intensive Care area, they found Bryan down on his hands and knees praying as a doctor and two nurses were attending to him. A couple minutes later the doctor came over to them and said "Folks, that was a very close call, but we managed to get out of immediate danger. I wish I could be more optimistic, but he's literally clinging to life at this moment. It's just a wait and see situation at this time." Bryan and Emily hugged and stood by his bedside for a few moments. Then all three went back to the waiting room and spent the entire night.

Another day and night passed with no significant change, and due to a shortage of beds in the intensive care unit, Christian was moved to a private room. A large reclining chair was placed in the corner of the room to sleep in for whichever family member was going stay the night.. Emily would stand at his bedside and touch his face and gently run her fingers through his wavy light brown hair, whispering softly into his ear. He was her first child, born when she had just turned nineteen, and she always felt in a way that they had grown up together.

With Emily stationed in the chair on Wednesday night, she was continually pondering memories of Christian's life, from important events and milestones to seemingly insignificant little occurrences. They seemed to come randomly, not necessarily in any type of chronological order, one after another. She loved watching the passion he devoted to his certain special interests, despite the fact that they were not common among boys his own age. He was reading books about coin collecting when he was seven and would often ask for a certain coin for a Christmas or birthday present. He started watching golf on television when he was nine and begged for a set of clubs.

But it was playing the cello that seemed to provide him with inner joy. Emily and her sister Jesse took him to see the Rhode Island Philharmonic Orchestra in Providence when he was ten, and he became transfixed with the cello player. He said to his mother "Mum.... Did I used to have one of those when I was little? It looks so familiar to me." She laughed and assured him that he never had any such thing. Though he had never shown any interest in playing a musical instrument, he kept asking over the next few days if he could get one and learn how to play. She finally relented and located a store in Providence that carried instruments such as violins, cellos, and stand-up basses, and took him there to look at them.

When a salesman approached them, she explained about his interest in learning, and while he looked a bit skeptical, he said, "Let me go grab an older used cello from out back and maybe he can see if it feels comfortable to him." A few moments later he brought out an older, slightly worn-looking cello and sat Christian in a chair and handed it to him along with a bow, and began to explain the proper technique.

Before the gentleman got very far in his instruction, Christian began displaying near perfect technique, gently swaying the bow across the strings and actually producing a melody that sounded pleasant. The salesman stood back with a stunned look. He asked Emily "Are you sure he's never played this instrument before?"

"I'm quite sure he's never been within fifty feet of one" she responded.

"It's really quite remarkable" he responded. He continued "I can give you a very good price on this particular instrument, and I can give you the name of a gentleman who gives private lessons."

Christian proudly walked out of the store with his cello and began his lessons a couple weeks later. After his third lesson, held at the instructor's home in Cranston, the cello teacher pulled her aside and told her Christian's progress was remarkable, and was like nothing he had ever seen in a student before. "I can't help but believe that he was born to be a cello player."

Emily sat in Christian's hospital room and smiled at the memory.

Then she recalled a silly little incident when he was eight and watching a couple hours of *The Three Stooges* episodes on television. He got a piece of paper and a pen and was writing on it while lying on the floor. When he was done, he brought the paper out to his mother in the kitchen and said "Mum, do you have the address for The Three Stooges? I wrote them a letter and asked them why they act so dumb."

Emily laughed and thought to herself, *The Stooges haven't been alive for decades.*

She gradually drifted off to sleep in the recliner with these thoughts on her mind.

3

―――――――

ON THE SEVENTH day, just as daylight was starting to break, Christian started to flutter his eyes.... very slowly at first, then more rapidly until they were open. After a few moments, he finally fully opened them and raised his head slightly. He looked down towards the foot of his bed and saw a vague image of a man. As he focused a bit more, he saw that it was a young man roughly his own age who also seemed to look a little bit like him. The man was dressed in some type of uniform that appeared to be that of a hotel clerk or a waiter. He began to speak very slowly, saying "Christian... you have been given a very special gift... It is very important that you use it very wisely... I will never be far away...."

With that, the image of the young man began to very gradually fade until it had disappeared completely. Christian was looking around the room and was completely confused. He was not sure if he had just woken from a dream. He saw his mother curled up on a big recliner in the corner of the room and started to call her. "Mum... Mum... Wake up!"

She started to stir, and when she finally opened her eyes to see her son awake, she shrieked "Christian! Are you really awake?" She ran over and hugged him and was hysterical. A moment later she ran out into the hallway and hollered for the nurse. Before two nurses came into the room, she quickly tried to explain to him what had happened to him, and how she never gave up hope.

Two nurses entered to get vital signs and observe his condition. As one was taking his temperature, he looked her straight in the eyes for about ten seconds and said to her, "Your mother is telling me to tell you she is very proud of you. She knew when she saw you playing nurse at seven years old that you were going to grow up to be one."

The nurse looked at him quizzically and replied, "My mother passed away four years ago."

"I know," Christian said, "but she just came to me and said that she wanted you to know that." Tears welled up in her eyes and she quickly walked out of the room. Christian then asked the other nurse present if a guy was in his room just a little while ago. She responded that no one had been in his room since she herself checked on him around three a.m.

His mother went over to him and asked, "What just went on with that nurse?"

"I just told her what I saw" he said, "And I thought she'd be happy." The remaining nurse came over and slipped a small device on his finger to check his oxygen level, and as he was looking at her, he said "You're going to buy that house you're looking at in Middletown, and you're going to live there a very long time. It's the one."

The nurse said to Emily "Can we speak out in the hallway for a minute?" Once outside the room, the nurse told Emily that physically it appears upon first check that he has returned completely to normal. "But neurologically, I wonder if something else is going on. I'm going to mention this to his doctor and see if he might want to order more tests."

"Yes... of course" Emily agreed. "We want to make sure everything is completely okay before we bring him home."

In the meantime, Emily had already called her husband with the news, and he and Shannon arrived. When they walked into his room, they both rushed to his bedside and gave him big hugs. Christian joked, "I guess I really beat the odds by getting hit by lightning huh?"

They all laughed, and his father said, "It was Mother Nature against you. And I think you won this one!"

His sister piped in. "You know, you used to sometimes annoy me at home, but I have to be honest... I've kind of missed having you around... mainly because I don't have anyone to make fun of," she said with a large grin.

Christian was looking at her as she spoke, and out of the blue he said to her, "You're going to graduate from Johnson and Wales University, so don't waste your time applying to other schools."

Shannon looked quizzically at her mother and said "Mum.... what is he talking about? Is the medication making him say weird things?'

As Bryan went to Christian's bedside and started talking

to him, Emily pulled Shannon aside and responded, "Well, he has said a few peculiar things since he woke up,but let's not worry about that right now. Let's just be happy he's finally back with us."

"But you know what's weird Mum?" Shannon added, "I've never mentioned one word to him about thinking about applying to Johnson and Wales... even though it is high on my list. How would he have any idea of such a thing?"

"It's puzzling, I know, she answered. "I'll have to talk to his doctor when he gets in."

A different nurse came in the room to briefly monitor a piece of equipment, and after watching her closely for a few moments, Christian said to her, "I see you'll have a nice time on your cruise in a couple of weeks."

The young nurse had a stunned look on her face and meekly said, "Thanks" as she walked out of the room.

The nurse in charge of the floor came in and told the family that they would have to wait out in the waiting room for a while, and that the doctor would be in to see Christian soon, and he would speak to them afterward.

Emily went over and gave him one more hug and whispered in his ear, "Honey... try to think about what you're saying to these people before you speak."

4

A SHORT TIME later, Dr. Bergman walked into Christian's room and said to him, "You are a very lucky young man. A lot of people don't survive what happened to you. You were in a coma for a week, and there were some scary moments along the way. I just want to check a few things." With that, the doctor put his stethoscope in his ears to check Christian's heartbeat, shined a light in his eyes, had him follow his fingers with his eyes, and inserted a scope in each ear. He then asked Christian if he had any pain or unusual feelings anywhere, to which he replied "No."

Dr. Bergman then said, "It has been reported to me by the nursing staff that you've made a few unusual comments to them. Can you explain a little bit about that?"

"Well," Christian began, "I guess I was just seeing these really strong images around them... and I felt like they should know and that I should tell them."

Br. Bergman then asked, "Have things like this happened to you before?"

"I would say, no, nothing like that" Christian answered. "But right now" Christian continued, "Your Grandpa Will would like me to tell you how much he enjoyed driving you around in his antique red Thunderbird convertible when you were about ten or twelve years old. You two would fly kites at Cape Brenton Point and go fishing off the rocks along Narragansett Bay.

The doctor was stunned at what he was hearing and didn't quite know how to react. He did not want to display any emotion in front of the young patient, but it had caught him off guard, and after a moment, he removed his glasses and dabbed his eyes. Christian continued with another message. "He is pleased that you still have the car and said that you should check the glove box. He created a false bottom and something is tucked underneath it for you, but he never got to tell you about it."

"That's quite an interesting story Christian, and I'm sure we'll get to discuss it in a little more depth later on. In the meantime, I'm going to arrange to have a few neurological tests done before we make any decisions. The good news is, so far, all indications are that physically you are completely back to normal." Dr. Bergman concluded by saying, "I'd like to go out now and update your parents on everything."

Dr. Bergman greeted the Casey family in the waiting room and asked them to come into a small office where they could speak privately. Once seated he began by telling them how miraculous it seemed that Christian would come out of his comatose state and have virtually no physical issues. The doctor informed them that his previous couple of experiences with patients struck by lightning were dramatically worse. He then expressed a bit of concern over a few interactions that occurred during his first hour of consciousness. He asked Emily and Bryan, "Have you ever known him to have some kind of unusual ability to see the future or the past, or to seem to communicate with people who have long passed away?"

"He's always been a pretty unique individual," Emily said, "but I don't believe we've ever seen anything like that."

Bryan added "I believe he's a very gifted young man, but not in that way that I ever recall seeing."

"Well," continued the doctor, "He's been saying things to people he doesn't know, including myself, that he has some unexplainable insight into people's past and futures." The doctor explained that he would like to call in a couple of neurologists and observe him closely over the next couple of days before they consider discharging him.

"Of course," Emily responded. "Under the circumstances that's perfectly understandable."

When Dr. Bergman arrived at his home in Bristol late that afternoon, he grabbed the keys to his late grandfather's antique Thunderbird and went out to the four-car garage in which it was parked. Based on what Christian had told him that morning, he checked the glove compartment. Feeling around inside it, he did find some type of false bottom he was unaware of, and lifting it up, he found an envelope. Inside were three one thousand dollar bills.

5

THE FOLLOWING DAY, two neurologists met Dr. Bergman at the hospital to meet and interview Christian. The previous afternoon he had undergone a couple of brain scan procedures, and the doctors were interested in looking over the results. Upon reviewing them with Dr. Bergman, Doctors Woodward and Mangini were surprised to find that there was no unusual activity.

Dr. Bergman brought them to Christian's room and introduced them to him. Each would have a few minutes one-on-one time with him to do a brief interview in order to get their initial impressions. Dr. Mangini was the first to have a few minutes in the room and started out by inquiring about the young man's family and general interests. When he found out Christian's passion for the cello, he told him that his sister had played the viola in an orchestra in Connecticut several years back.

Suddenly Christian looked at him rather blankly and said,

"The house you own in Florida is going to be damaged severely by a hurricane."

Trying hard not to appear shocked that the young man would even know that he owned a house in Florida, the doctor asked him, "Can you describe to me how that thought came to you?"

Christian responded "I've been wondering about these things myself since yesterday. Sometimes it seems that when I focus on someone, an image about them just seems to appear in front of me." He continued, "With your house.... It sort of came in two quick parts... In the first ...I saw a house getting damaged by severely high winds ... and then it quickly switched to you walking around it after looking at the terrible damage." He added, "I'm not sure how I can explain that I knew where it was."

Then Christian asked Dr. Mangini, "Do you think this has something to do with what happened to me last week?"

He replied "That's something the other doctors and I will have to discuss. You and I will talk again." And with that he exited the room.

A few moments later, Dr. Woodward entered the room. Trying to put a casual tone on their conversation, the doctor remarked that he had heard Christian was an outstanding golfer and expressed his own love for the game. They discussed a few technical aspects of the sport until Christian interrupted and said, "Your dad wants to tell you that you should visit Uncle Earl soon.... that he's been on his own for a while and that he needs some help."

Smiling, Dr. Woodward thanked him for reminding him

and assured him he would do that over the upcoming week-end. "My Dad's been gone for a few years," the doctor added, "but it's good to know he's still looking out for us." After a bit more conversation, the doctor was set to sit with the others and discuss his theory of what Christian was experiencing.

Once the three doctors were seated back in Dr. Bergman's office, Dr. Woodward began. "I believe the young man is showing signs of at least some form of *Acquired Savant Syndrome.* Of course, it's very rare and has only been documented in less than three dozen patients after serious head trauma."

Dr. Mangini added, "Yes, I remember reading the case of a young man who, once he recovered, walked over to a piano and started playing like a virtuoso, even though he had no prior knowledge."

Said Dr. Bergman, "I think this is the closest we can come to explaining the boy's new-found abilities. Now at least I have something reasonably definitive to tell his parents."

"Speaking of his parents," said Dr. Woodward, "I'd like to get their approval on the possibility of doing an article on his specific case for one of the medical journals I contribute to on occasion."

"One other thing you might do Dr. Bergman." said Dr. Mangini, "is to have his parents try to convince the boy that he doesn't have to share these images he sees with every person he encounters. Not everyone is going to respond well to hearing something about their future, or a visit from a deceased relative."

"Good point." replied Dr. Bergman.

6

LATER THAT AFTERNOON, Dr. Bergman met with the Casey family to inform them of the diagnosis that the neurologists agreed upon. He explained in detail about Acquired Savant Syndrome and discussed a few case histories. He tried to get them to realize that his condition was likely permanent, and life for him would never quite be normal as it was before. The Caseys were all quite taken back by this aspect of the condition.

"As the doctors and I discussed" he told them, "however difficult it may be, he may have to find a way to keep that ability under wraps a little bit. It's likely that not everyone he encounters will be open to hearing his predictions, or his contact with their relatives who've passed on." He concluded, "I may be able to suggest a counselor who would work with him on that."

Looking over at her husband, Emily answered 'Yes... whatever it takes to allow him to have some semblance of a normal life."

With regards to Christian's discharge from the hospital, he felt the medical staff should observe him for another couple of days, and that if no issues arose, he would be able to go home on Sunday afternoon. The doctor then added one note of caution. "I'm going to suggest that if you are ever contacted by the media wanting to tell his story and write about his very unusual condition, that you decline and give no detail," he advised. "If this becomes public knowledge, he is going to be inundated with requests for readings and sessions where he predicts the outcomes of events, and he will never have a moment's peace." He concluded, "He would be viewed as a freak of nature and a sideshow."

Bryan responded, "We may not have realized that outcome until it was too late. Thank you for the warning." With that, the family departed and tried to come to terms with how Christian's day to day life might be affected.

The following day, a young kitchen worker wheeled Christian's lunch on a cart into his room. Word had gotten around to staff members about his abilities, and the young woman looked around to make sure no one was listening and asked Christian, "I know I shouldn't do this, but I wonder if you'd be able to give me some advice?"

The fact that she was extremely good looking prompted Christian to be a bit more accommodating than he might normally be, and he asked what her question was.

She then said, "Can you tell if I have any kind of future with my current boyfriend?"

He looked her deep in the eyes for nearly ten seconds, and

responded, "I see you in a wedding gown, exchanging vows with a guy."

She then pulled a cell phone out of the pocket of her smock and located a photo, which she then showed to him. "Does the guy in your vision look like this guy?"

"No," he replied. "Not at all. The guy I see has very dark, curly hair and is very thin."

With a disappointed look on her face, she simply said, "I guess I'm going to have to reconsider this relationship," and walked out of the room.

Late that night at around two in the morning, Christian woke to find the vision of the young man who had visited him a few days before again standing near the foot of his bed. He began to speak, with a statement similar to his first, saying, "Don't abuse your wonderful gift... use it only for good."

Christian tried to say, "wait... wait....", but the image faded quickly. He believed in his heart however that this would not be the last time he experienced this mysterious figure.

7

SUNDAY MORNING ARRIVED and it was now his eleventh day in the hospital. Dr. Bergman had given his approval for Christian's discharge, and he would be going home shortly after lunch. His family arrived shortly before noon, all with big smiles on their faces. Emily had feared during the darkest moments that this time would never come, and she was eternally grateful. She and Christian thanked the nursing staff for all of their care and kindness. Bryan had taken a classic Rolls Royce from his dealership to give Christian a ride home in style, and he felt like a celebrity as he took his place in the back seat. "Driver, maybe you should drop me off at the Vanderbilt mansion on Bellevue Ave.," he joked to his dad.

As soon as he got home, he ran to his room and played a few passages on his cello, then took his golf clubs out into the backyard and took a few practice swings.

In the back of his mind, he was wondering how frequently his new ability would show itself spontaneously and perhaps interfere with his day-to-day life. He wondered if it was something he could have some control over and simply tune out if it happened at inopportune or inconvenient moments.

That evening there was a relatively harmless occurrence when he was watching a movie with his father. Christian was focused on the actor on the screen, when he suddenly asked Bryan, "Dad... who is that actor?"

"His name is James Fiorentini," his dad answered, "and I actually think he lives in Connecticut."

Christian then stated, "He's going to buy a Ferrari from you and he's going to do a local television ad for your dealership."

"Well, that will be nice publicity," said a pleased Bryan, glancing over at Emily with a quizzical expression.

They made the decision that Christian would enjoy a couple of days off and then return to school for the final week-and-a-half of his senior year.

He was very pleased to be sleeping in his own bed once again, but during his third night home, it became clear that his mysterious hospital visitor had followed him. At about two a.m. on Wednesday morning, he woke to find the young man standing by his bedside. Speechless, Christian stared at him until he gradually began to hear the words. "The time is coming near for you to learn of our unbreakable connection... we have had the same blood running through our veins."

It was a brief encounter, but it set Christian on a whole new path of curiosity as to who this person was, and what role he may have played in his life. Based on his statement, he could be either a relative or an ancestor—but how far back might he go? What information might he share? There seemed to be more questions than answers at this point. All he could do was wait for the next encounter and hope for more detail.

He finally drifted back off to sleep, and he awoke at 6:45 and prepared for his first day back at school.

He pulled into his parking space in a BMW two-seater from his father's dealership, and as he walked in, he was greeted by cheers and slaps on the back from fellow classmates, as well as hugs from several girls. He felt like a celebrity, but deep in his mind he was wondering how his new gifts might come into play, and how much it may interrupt with his general focus. He had not been around this many people at one time in a while, and realizing his fears, it brought a flood of images around several students and teachers.

In first period English class, he was talking to Kaley Domineaux who was sitting beside him and saw an image playing out in front of him. She was singing on a theater stage dressed in a costume in some type of play. He knew she had a passion for acting and was pleased to see that she would go on to some level of success. He also wisely knew that telling her about it would prompt more questions that he did not care to try to explain.

A while later in third period algebra class, seated in the front row, he was focused on his middle-aged teacher Mrs. Corrigan. A vision appeared beside her of her late mother, telling Christian to tell her that she wished she had been here to see the birth of her great-granddaughter, and that it would have been so nice if the four generations could have spent a little time together. "Just let her know I'm there" the old woman said.

Christian simply couldn't resist the temptation to pass on this connection. As class ended and the rest of the students filed out of the room, he approached the teacher's desk. He said to her "I received a message from your mom." He then related it to her as concisely as possible and added, "Please don't ask questions... and let's never speak of this again." He then walked out of the room. Mrs. Corrigan sat there stunned as tears welled up in her eyes.

There were a few more incidents throughout the school day. During a conversation at lunch with his longtime friend Jared Cushman, he saw him pushing twin toddlers in a baby carriage down the street. Christian did not want to spoil that surprise.

When he got home from school, he was so mentally exhausted that he took a two-hour nap. He felt his brain had worked overtime, and he was hoping this wasn't a sign of things to come. At dinner, his parents asked him about his first day back and he tried to downplay what he had experienced, simply saying that sitting in school all day was very tiring. In his heart, he wasn't looking forward to a repeat the following day.

It turned out to be more of the same, with highlights and sad revelations. Talking to class valedictorian Nathan Rigolsby, he saw him, around twenty years older, being sworn in as a United States senator for Rhode Island. His contact with fellow golf team member Ryan Landreau produced the image of Ryan's gravestone, which showed that he had nine years to live. With that, he felt he had to get away and went out to the parking lot to sit in his car. He had no desire to be around people and what contact with them might show.

He left to go home an hour early and retired to his room. He sat there in silence, and when he didn't come down for dinner, both of his parents came to check on him. When they asked if something was wrong, Christian broke down. Through tears, he said, "I don't think I can go through this every day. I see things that I have to keep inside.... things I don't want to know." Emily gave him a hug as Bryan was rubbing his back.

His mother said, "I think we should call Dr. Bergman and arrange to have you meet with the counselor he talked about. Maybe they can help you find a way to deal with this." Christian responded that he would be open to anything that might help.

The entire ordeal had been a roller coaster ride for Emily. She saw her boy go from the brink of death to being perfectly physically healthy in a week's time, and now she couldn't bear to see him in such emotional angst. Her children and her family were her entire life. She had basically been a stay-at-home mom until the kids reached their teens, and theirs and Bryan's needs always came first. She pledged to call Dr. Bergman in the morning.

In the meantime, Christian would try to struggle through one more day of school before the weekend arrived. He was looking forward to dropping by his father's auto dealership on Saturday to familiarize himself with some of the latest additions to the high-end foreign auto inventory. In a week-and-a-half, he would become a permanent full-time employee there, set to work his way up the ladder. His new abilities, however, may yet provide him with other opportunities.

8

CHRISTIAN'S SCHOOL DAY on Friday was fairly uneventful as he tried hard to avoid contact with people or look them in the eye. He had come to the conclusion that close contact was the trigger that would lead to many of these paranormal experiences.

He went to his father's auto dealership on Saturday morning for the first time since the incident. He spent the day cleaning and preparing three recent additions to be shown: a Mercedes, a Jaguar, and a Range Rover. He thankfully had minimal contact with others while there.

That night while sleeping, he was awakened in the wee hours by the image of the young man who had visited him twice sitting at the end of the edge of his bed. Before Christian could say anything, the figure became fully clear and said "Christian... it is time for you to learn the truth about our connection. Let me start at the very beginning." Christian sat up slightly and focused his eyes on the young man's face. He continued, "My name is Andrew. It was the summer of 2007, and your mother Emily was my girlfriend. I was set to go away to college in Pennsylvania for my freshman year in a week. We had just found out a week before that she was pregnant. We didn't know what to do, but my parents insisted that I begin the school year. I didn't want to leave her, but I didn't know what choice I had." Christian continued to listen silently.

He continued, "It was a Thursday night, and I had just finished my shift at the restaurant I was working at, and I was walking out to my car. From here, let me take you there, and show you exactly what happened." At that moment, Christian's entire field of vision appeared like a movie screen. He saw a large parking lot with several cars, and Andrew exiting the building wearing his waiter's uniform. As he was about to arrive at his car, a man got out of a pickup truck and walked over to him. At this point Andrew said to Christian, "You'll recognize that man as your grandfather Dan—your mother's father."

Christian continued to watch, and saw his grandfather begin hollering at Andrew, saying, "You know you're going to have to be a man and marry Emily."

Andrew said to him, "I'm not in any position to do that right now... I have to leave for school next week."

"I don't give a damn about your school," Dan shouted, you've got an obligation here. Be a man."

Andrew responded, "My parents are insisting that I go."

Grabbing Andrew by the shirt, Dan said, "Here's something to help change your mind," as he punched him in the face. "And I've got one for your father, too," and he struck another blow. The second one sent Andrew to the ground quickly, and he hit his head hard on the curbstone. He lay there motionless as blood started pouring out on the pavement.

Dan looked around to see if there were any witnesses to what had just occurred, and seeing no one, he walked quickly to his truck and drove away.

Andrew interjected to Christian, "This is when my soul rose up and was looking down on my dead body. I was a month away from my nineteenth birthday."

"But there's more," Andrew said as Christian continued to watch. A moment later, a young local man came cutting through the parking lot and saw Andrew lying on the ground, completely still. He looked all around, and seeing no one, he reached down and pulled the wallet out of Andrew's pants pocket. Just at that moment a police car was slowly driving by, and seeing a body lying on the ground, pulled the cruiser over, with two officers getting out to investigate. They immediately recognized the man standing there as someone who had several previous brushes with the local police. He began to run, but one officer pulled his service handgun and ordered him to stop. Realizing he had nowhere to escape to, the man stopped and put his hands up. The other officer radioed for backup and asked for an ambulance to be sent to the scene.

As the officer searched the man at the scene, he came across the wallet that he had taken from Andrew with his license in it along with forty dollars. The man, later identified as Willy Pinto, was placed under arrest and taken into custody. Andrew was later pronounced dead at the scene by the medical examiner. Despite his denials, Pinto was charged with murder.

The entire scene disappeared from Christian's view and only Andrew was left to speak. He said, "So as you've likely been able to figure out... I am your biological father... and I was killed by your grandfather... though someone else paid the price." He concluded, "Use your gifts wisely, my son." His image then very slowly began to fade until Christian was left alone to ponder what had just been revealed to him.

He lay awake in bed for an hour trying to review this unimaginable turn of events.

His mind was flooded with questions and curiosity about what just transpired. He got out of bed and got on his computer. He started by attempting to research the murder of the young man who was claiming to be his father. He did a simple search using the words *Rhode Island murder, August 2007, Willy Pinto – Andrew.*

Sure enough, he located an article in the *Providence Journal* newspaper from that time titled, "Newport man arrested for the murder of Portsmouth teen." It identified the murdered man as 18-year-old Andrew Van Buren and detailed what was known at the time. It went on to say that Pinto was arraigned in Newport District Court and held without bail.

He continued to do more searches and found that Pinto was found guilty of second-degree murder in February of 2008 and sentenced to life at Rhode Island's Adult Correctional Institution. He would be eligible for parole in twenty years.

Christian's world was turned upside down. In the past couple of hours, he learned that his biological father was not the man he thought, that he had been killed by his grandfather, and that an innocent man was serving time for the murder. It was going to take a while to digest all this, and to have any idea how to proceed.

9

WITH HIS MIND racing, Christian wasn't able to fall back asleep until about 5 a.m. Finally, at just a bit before noon, Emily came in to check on him. She found him awake, staring blankly at the ceiling, seeming oblivious to her presence. She broke the silence by saying, "Boy... your busy day at the dealership yesterday must have wiped you out."

He finally looked over at her and said "You know ...I thought when I came home from the hospital it was sort of like the first day of my new life. But with what I experienced last night... today might be."

"Well......what do you mean by that?" his mother asked. "What happened?"

"I had another one of these...visits...I guess you'd call them," he replied. "But this one was a real eye opener... a real game changer."

"So... can you describe it to me?" she asked.

"I can try," he answered..." but you better sit down."

"Well, for starters.... I met my biological father.... And as you know... it's not Bryan Casey."

With a stunned look on her face, she said, "Oh my God Christian... I know I should have told you a long time ago... let me try to explain."

"Before you start," Christian interrupted, "I know that he was murdered before I was born."

"Okay." she began. "I started seeing Bryan a few months after this all happened. He was there for me when I was in the hospital and supported me every step of the way. He treated you like his own from your very first day and immediately became your dad." She had to collect herself for a moment and then continued. "We got married a few months later and he adopted you almost immediately. He's been the perfect Dad.... always there for you. And when your sister Shannon was born a couple years later, we felt like we were blessed with the perfect little family."

She concluded, "I know I should have found a way to tell you... but I hope this doesn't change anything."

Christian assured her that it wouldn't and decided to keep the rest of the story to himself for a while.

A while after dinner, in the early evening, Bryan knocked on Christian's bedroom door and was told to come in. He sat down at Christian's desk and asked, "Can we talk?"

Christian answered, "Sure, Dad."

Bryan answered, "I can't tell you how good it is to hear you call me Dad," with a smile. Christian assured him "You will always be my dad. No one could have been better at that than you've been."

Bryan told him, "It was a joy to watch you grow and be involved in every aspect of your life. Cub Scouts, Little League, all of your various interests, watching you progress as a cello player and a golfer....Being a dad to both you and your sister has been one of the joys of my life."

"There will be a lot more," Christian added, as they hugged each other.

All seemed well for the time being, but as the evening wore on, Christian couldn't stop thinking about the man in prison all these years for a murder he did not commit. Over the next couple of days, he did as much research as the internet would allow and found as a matter of public record that Willy Pinto was still serving time in the Rhode Island maximum security prison roughly a half hour away. Christian pondered the idea of writing him a letter and explaining to him what he knew. He also realized it would be quite a challenge to explain how he knew what he knew without sounding like an insane individual.

He would become preoccupied with the project, writing and re-writing the letter several times over the next week.

10

CHRISTIAN RETURNED TO school Monday morning for what would be his final week. He was going to try his best to maintain the strategy of avoiding close contact with others to keep his visions and visits to a minimum. He lapsed a bit during western civilization class and was focused on his teacher, Mrs. Backlund. In a vision he saw her name on a placard on the office of the school's principal. He couldn't resist having a little fun with her as he was filing out of class.

As he passed her, he said, "In a few years, you're going to be the principal of this school."

She responded, "Well Mr. Casey, tell me how you know that?"

"Well" he answered, "I'm not sure you'd believe me.... But I'm pretty sure you're going to remember this moment when you get hired."

The following day, he was walking in the corridor and walking toward him was fellow senior Mark Hendricks. The image of his twin brother, who died in an accident two years earlier, was walking beside him. Christian had to keep this one to himself.

These incidents continued to occur randomly, although it seemed to require him to focus and concentrate on a particular person, however briefly. Oftentimes the glimpses into the future were not easy to identify exactly when they would occur. His mother had made an appointment for the following week with the counselor recommended by Dr. Bergman, and he hoped it might be helpful.

His school year concluded on Friday without any significant or upsetting occurrences, and he was relieved to put this chapter of his life behind him. He had long felt like a bit of an outsider among his peers, and that there was something just a bit different about him in the way that he thought and the interests toward which he gravitated. His final obligation would be to attend his graduation ceremony in three weeks and then he could get on with the pursuit of his goals and dreams.

By the following day he felt that he had composed an effective letter to Willy Pinto that might open a dialogue between the two. He tried to keep it simple in hopes that he would have a further opportunity to delve deeper into the details. The letter read:

> *Mr. Pinto,*
>   *My name is Christian Casey, and I am an eighteen-year-old who is graduating from Portsmouth High School in a few weeks. I have recently learned that*

you were found guilty in 2008 of the murder of my biological father Andrew Van Buren six months before I was born.

I have also learned that you were not the person who committed the murder, and that the jury made a mistake in finding you guilty.

I am willing to do whatever I can to convince the authorities of your innocence and have you released as soon as possible. I would be willing to come to visit you at your facility if you care to discuss this further.

Christian Casey

Christian read the letter over several times and was convinced that this simple approach was the best way to start this project. He addressed an envelope and mailed it on Monday morning. He then headed off to his father's auto dealership for his first day as a permanent full-time employee.

He was also giving thought to his next steps toward getting serious about pursuing a career as a professional cello player in an orchestra and entering local golf tournaments. He had always been a driven individual and knew that progress in any endeavor required aggressive action and determination. These things weren't simply going to come to him.

11

THE FOLLOWING SATURDAY he checked the mailbox and found a letter addressed to him with name Willy Pinto up in the left-hand corner. Though he was hoping for some response, he was shocked to actually see it and couldn't wait to read the contents. He rushed to his room, closed the door, and tore open the envelope.

It read:

> *Christian,*
>
> *I was completely stunned to read your letter. I have no idea how you know what you know, but the one thing I do know is that you're correct. If you can convince the authorities and get me released, I will owe you more than I can ever pay. If you would like to come to visit me and tell me the whole story, that would be okay.*
>
> *Willy Pinto*

Christian felt like the very first hurdle in the project was cleared, but there would be a long way to go, and this was going to require an intense amount of thought, legwork, and persuasion.

He checked into the visiting hours at the Adult Correctional Institution in Cranston and planned to go there on Tuesday evening. He did not want his parents to know anything about what he was doing and told them he was going to a music store in Providence to buy a set of cello strings and a new bow. When he arrived at the prison, he was awed by the fortress-like appearance of the more than century-old stone structure. He had to fill out a visitation form, get searched for contraband, and get electronically buzzed in through several heavy steel locked doors one at a time. He felt completely out of his element. It was an environment of which he was completely unfamiliar and was extremely unsettling. Halfway in, he wanted to turn back and ask the correction officer to let him back out, but he knew he wanted to meet Pinto. He was finally escorted to a visiting room where he sat and waited for ten minutes, discreetly glancing around as inmates were sitting across tables from their visitors.

Finally, Willy entered the room and was instructed by the escorting officer where to sit. As the fortyish man with shoulder length black hair who appeared to be of Hispanic descent took his seat, he said, "So I assume you must be Christian. No one else who fits your description would ever come to visit me" he chuckled. "Yes, Mr. Pinto, it's nice to finally meet you." he responded. "You can call me Willy .... no need to be formal in here."

"So, I'd like to get right to it" Willy said. "Tell me exactly how you know what you know."

"Okay... but this is going to be one of the strangest stories you ever heard," said Christian.

He went right back to the beginning about getting struck by lightning. Willy interjected that he remembers seeing that on the news a few weeks back. "That was *you* man?" he exclaimed.

"Yeah" said Christian, "But that's just the beginning." He talked about being in a coma for a week, and that when he came out of it, something was very different. He detailed some of the experiences he began having and told of the doctor's rare diagnosis of Acquired Savant Syndrome.

"As I'm telling you this" Christian said, "your grandfather Pedro is standing behind you, telling you to listen to me."

"Holy shit" said Willy... for real?"

"I promise I would never say anything that I was not experiencing," Christian said. He added, "He is telling me that you used to help him when he was working on his old pickup truck, and when he was putting that addition on his little house in Pawtucket."

"I'm sold, man" Willy said. "You couldn't possibly know this stuff."

"So," Christian continued, "I got a visit from my father, and he was able to show me the entire scene when his murder occurred. I saw who did it... and I know it wasn't you."

"Well... you're right," said Willy. "One of the strangest things I've ever heard. But" he added, "How are we going to convince a district attorney to re-open my case based on your visions? He might laugh you out of his office."

"Well," said Christian, "I'm going to have to give that a lot of thought and come up with a strategy. I want you to know... I can be very persistent and pretty persuasive when I want to be." He concluded, "And I can be a little obsessive with things... so when I take on a quest, I get pretty determined."

"Okay," responded Willy, "but until you start making some kind of progress...I'm not gonna get my hopes up too high." Christian assured him that he understood that.

Christian then changed the subject and said to Willy, "While I'm here, I'd like to get to know a little bit about you.... your background... things like that."

"Well," he started, "I actually had a pretty decent child-hood. My grandparents came over from Portugal way back, and we all lived in Pawtucket. I wasn't too bad of a student and graduated from Pawtucket High School in 2003. I moved to Newport after school and got a halfway decent job, but after about a year the place went out of business. That's when things started to go downhill for me."

Willy went on to explain that he fell in with the wrong crowd and started drinking a lot. Aside from a couple other minor scrapes with the law, he beat up a guy pretty badly and ended up spending a year in the county house of correction for it.

"So, when I got arrested for that murder, my previous record didn't do me any favors."

Christian said, "It must be unbearable to be serving time for something you know you didn't do."

"Well," replied Willy, "I was extremely hostile and resent-ful for a very long time, obviously. I tried a few appeals through my attorney, but none of them went anywhere. I just considered myself a victim of a very flawed judicial system. I have considered suicide many, many times, but thankfully, something prevented me from going through with it. I'm eligible for parole in a little over a year, so I'm putting some hope in that possibility."

"So where do you stand right now, emotionally?" Christian asked. Just as Willy was about to respond, Christian interrupted "Wait... I need to tell you that I just had a very clear vision of you... just a little bit older than you are right now... standing at a podium talking to a large crowd of people in some type of hall or auditorium. You're holding up a book and referring to something in it."

"Jesus man," Willy said with a stunned look on his face. "I'm witnessing your gift right here as we speak."

"It's indicating to me that there is life for you after this place," assured Christian.

"I can't tell you how good that is to hear," said Willy.

"So, what I was about to tell you" Willy continued, "...was that I had a cellmate about six or seven years ago who was able to completely change my attitude and way of looking at things. He was a black guy who had a horrible early life and went through many terrible things. But somehow, he was able to keep his sanity and had an amazing outlook on things. He taught me a lot and I am a far better, more mature person for knowing him," he concluded.

"Well," said Christian, "I think I'm going to be a better person for knowing you, and it's time for me to get to work on this."

With that they concluded their visit, and Christian told Willy he would be in touch.

12

ON HIS DRIVE back home, it occurred to Christian that he had heard of occasions where psychics were utilized by law enforcement agencies to help solve crimes. It was time for him to research these and find specific examples of it being a legitimate option. If he could convince people in positions of power to believe what he had seen, there would be no reason to keep Willy incarcerated.

It also occurred to him that in revealing that Willy was innocent, he may be asked to reveal who the real killer was. This would present a major dilemma.

He had always thought the world of his Grandpa Dan, and the vision he was shown seemed terribly uncharacteristic of him. To Christian's knowledge, his grandfather never had as much as a speeding ticket and seemed to be the paragon of virtue. He almost certainly didn't intend to kill Andrew, and it was in all likelihood more of a freak outcome. If his grandfather was exposed by Christian as being responsible for someone's death and faced criminal charges at his now advanced age, how might that all play out? How would he be viewed by relatives and friends if his actions culminated in his grandfather serving time in prison, all for the purpose of freeing a man who had been a complete stranger, regardless of what was technically the right thing to do?

This was an aspect Christian would struggle with as he tried to formulate a strategy for moving forward.

He decided to look into the prospect of attempting to meet with the Newport County district attorney to see if he was even open to such a conversation. Now was a time to print out specific examples of the most compelling cases where psychics and mediums have had an influence on criminal cases and have them ready to refer to in the event of such a meeting. He knew that the law looked favorably upon a precedent being set. He had to be prepared. He knew he was going to be met with a great deal of skepticism and had to be ready with responses that were difficult to dispute.

He subsequently discovered at least a dozen gifted people who had assisted police departments in solving crimes and finding missing persons. One such woman from New Jersey had been involved in more than 4,000 investigations. Another could communicate with the dead and helped discover the circumstances of various deaths. This all gave Christian hope that his gifts were going to aid the cause significantly. He began working on a letter to the D.A. to request a meeting regarding the murder of Andrew Van Buren.

13

GRADUATION DAY HAD finally arrived and Christian was looking forward to putting it all behind him. There was a certain sense of joy in the event however, as he had plenty of friends he had known most of his life to share it with. He arranged to pick three of them up to arrive at the ceremony in grand style. His father allowed him to borrow a vintage silver Mercedes limousine from his dealership, and as they pulled up to the school, dozens and dozens of fellow students crowded around, some of them cheering as the boys got out. It made quite an impression.

A while later as they were standing around in their caps and gowns waiting to make their entrance, Christian was standing among a group of them. One of the male students said to Christian, "I've got to tell you man... you have to be the most unusual guy I know. You always drive some car that makes you look like the prince of some country in Europe. Most young guys like to play the guitar or the drums... and you play the cello. Most of us love football and basketball...

and you love golf. You have a coin collection that is better than my grandfather's." He concluded "Where did you come from, man?"

Christian wasn't quite sure if it was a compliment or an insult but tried to be good natured about it as several of the others present were laughing. He thought for a few seconds and said "Well... honestly... I think I'm sort of an 'old soul'. I guess I'm sort of a throwback... and maybe should have been born eighty years ago."

Another responded, "I think you may be on to something there Gramps," as they all laughed.

At several points throughout the ceremony Christian saw images of deceased grandparents stand beside their graduates. When class president Stuart White was giving his speech, a very clear image came of him being interviewed years later on television about a documentary he had made about the history of artificial intelligence.

When Christian walked across the stage to receive his diploma, his father Andrew was standing behind the principal.

After the ceremony, his parents had a small family party for him for mostly grandparents, aunts, uncles, and cousins. His mother had privately pulled the guests aside and asked them not to ask Christian to predict their future or give them a medium-type reading. Christian felt a bit awkward around his grandfather Dan and generally tried to avoid him. He was having difficulty coming to terms with what he now knew.

At one point he was looking at his 19-year-old cousin Kristi across the room, and after a moment, said to his Aunt Jesse standing beside him, "You better start saving up for a wedding." Knowing full well of his gift, Jesse smiled, shook her head and said, "Thanks for the warning."

Later on, after all had left, Christian decided to ride over to fellow graduate Garrett Stanley's party. He was surprised to find that there were at least a hundred classmates there, and when he walked in, one said "Here comes Prince Christian!" as laughter erupted through the room. He chatted briefly with a few, and a while later as he was sitting in the corner surveying the room, he had a vision of chaos erupting, fights breaking out, and bottles flying. He decided to slip out quietly and drive home.

His mother would tell him the following day that she heard there was a massive brawl at the party, the police were called, and three students were arrested.

That night in bed, contemplating his graduation day, he couldn't stop thinking about the comment his classmate had made about him being such an unusual person. For a very long time he had been aware of how different he felt from so many of his peers, and while he had no shortage of friends, he never quite felt like he fit in well with them. So often he seemed to gravitate towards things that were not typical of those his own age. These thoughts kept swirling in his head until he finally drifted off to sleep.

At some point in the middle of the night he woke to see an image of a man standing near his bed. This time, it was not the image of his father Andrew, but a man he had never seen before.

As the image became more in focus, he saw what appeared to be a middle-aged man dressed in a black tuxedo with blond hair and a very neatly manicured beard. He walked slowly around the room, looking at different things, and stopped to look at Christian. He then spoke. "When I was here, I was called Mason Harrington. I left far too soon, and I missed my existence. I had more to do. After a while, I found you and was able to start again."

The image then turned and started walking away, appearing to fade as he walked through the wall of Christian's bedroom.

In all the otherworldly experiences he had in the past couple of months, this one would take its place as the most puzzling and mysterious. It left him wide awake and trying to recreate the entire experience over and over that in reality probably lasted about thirty seconds. The only seemingly definitive piece of information was that the man's name was Mason Harrington.

This sent Christian to his computer to do a search to see if he could find anything.

He entered the name, and the search returned three people in the United States with that name, but apparently all still seemed to be alive. He refined to search to include the word *obituary* and an entry showed "Mason M. Harrington Obituary, 57, October 3, 2007, New York, N.Y." He clicked on the obituary and started to read.

It stated that Mr. Harrington was born in 1949 in Greenwich, Connecticut, and was struck and killed by an automobile in Manhattan. It went on to say that he was a cello player who played in the New York Philharmonic orchestra for twenty-two years. It added details about him such that Mason was an avid golfer since he was a teenager, had a passion for collecting coins, and also possessed a love for antique foreign automobiles.

This information left him shaking with tears streaming down his face. It would seem to explain so much. It was difficult given everything to not conclude that he may have essentially been reincarnated from Mason Harrington. Everything seemed to fit into place. They shared so many things, and as puzzling as it seemed when he spoke, it now made sense. Mason had said, "I left to soon... I missed my existence... I found you... I was able to start again."

What else could that mean? Christian thought. It instantly seemed pretty clear cut. Given everything that had happened to him recently, he knew more than ever that not everything had a universally accepted rational scientific explanation. There was far more at work to our existence. He himself was living proof.

Christian printed out the obituary and tucked it into his new high school yearbook on the page that featured his senior class photo.

At that point he went to work researching reincarnation. He read some and then did a search on *most compelling case histories of people who may have been reincarnated.* It was fascinating reading and actually comforted him to know that he may not be a total freak of nature after all. So many questions he had about himself now seemed to have a reason that he never before considered. After much pondering, he concluded that the reincarnation had nothing to do with his new gift, but that these new powers allowed him to make the contact that in turn allowed him to learn about his past life and how it influenced and shaped him.

14

THE FOLLOWING DAY, he began looking into contacting the Newport County district attorney, finding his name and the address
of his office. He then went to work composing a letter explaining the murder of his biological father and the information he
possessed that might exonerate the man serving time for it. He
requested a brief meeting at the D.A.'s convenience and promised to explain what he knew in detail. Looking ahead to that
potential meeting, he was quite certain that the D.A. would be
skeptical. He arrived upon the idea that he could possibly have
Dr. Bergman write a letter that would confirm the diagnosis
that he and two neurologists agreed upon in Christian's case
that might lend far more credibility to his claims. He stopped
by the doctor's office to officially make that request and was
told it would be mailed to him within a week.

A couple of days later, he finally went to his appointment
with the psychiatric counselor that Dr. Bergman had recommended. He sat down with Dr. Nicole Wahlstrom and she told

him his doctor had filled her in with the main details. She listened intently after asking him to elaborate on the finer details on how it was affecting him.

She went on to offer suggestions for when he preferred not to have an experience, such as strategies that would possibly create a diversion, thinking of certain keywords and phrases at that precise moment.

In the end, he felt the session was helpful and therapeutic. It was a pleasure to be able to open up so completely with someone who had some understanding and would not be remotely judgmental.

That evening, he was finally able to put the finishing touches on the letter to the district attorney. He mailed it the following morning and hoped for the best. Thinking about the prospect of this meeting throughout the day, he realized that he wished he could view the scene Andrew showed him again of how it all transpired so many years ago. Seeing it again, he could view far more detail, and maybe, just maybe it might contain some small detail he didn't notice the first time that could help him come closer to proving that the vision he was shown was completely accurate.

That night he laid awake in bed thinking deeply about it, and how he might recapture that visit from Andrew and what he had been shown. Perhaps his powers could bring it back. He concentrated deep and hard to the point that he had almost put himself into some type of trance. After what seemed like an hour, he saw a vague fluttering image that very slowly started to become clear. He was there—he had the same view of the parking lot on that fateful night. Without a visit from Andrew, he had been able to take himself there to witness it once again. He became hyper-focused, trying to absorb every minor detail in hopes that there was something that would be useful to him.

Everything was the same—Andrew exiting the restaurant, Grandpa Dan getting out of his truck, the shouting, the first punch, then the second punch that sent Andrew down hard to the pavement. But as Andrew was lying motionless, Christian happened to notice just off to the right a dark green Subaru wagon. He could see and read the Rhode Island license plate—number GC-3091. He instantly realized that this seemingly insignificant detail could hold a key. If, when telling of his vision to the district attorney he was having doubts about the validity of the story, Christian could introduce this detail.

As he slowly regained full consciousness after the vision concluded, he reached for a pen and jotted that license plate number down. He knew that the Rhode Island Registry of Motor Vehicles would have old records of to whom that vehicle was registered. If it came down to it, that person could be contacted and asked if he was at the restaurant that night. With a murder having occurred there while the person was inside, it no doubt would be something they would remember, even years later.

He felt he was in possession of compelling evidence that would prove his vision was historically accurate and that Willy Pinto was not responsible for his father's death. And now it was just a matter of waiting until he had the chance to reveal it.

15

CHRISTIAN HAD BEEN wrestling with the idea of talking to his grandfather about what he now knew. It was an extremely painful prospect. They had always had a wonderful relationship and there was never a harsh word spoken between them. He ultimately decided that his grandfather should be aware of the project he was undertaking on behalf of Willy.

Christian dropped by his house on Saturday afternoon and found him cutting wood on a table saw in the garage for some small piece of furniture he was building. They exchanged small talk for a few minutes, and then Christian said "Grandpa ... Let's sit down. I've got something pretty serious I want to talk to you about."

Emily had already explained to her parents about Christian's new condition, so the idea of the abilities he now possessed was not unknown to Dan. Christian started by giving a few specific examples of some of the experiences he had been having over the past couple of months, hoping to lend a bit of credibility to the bomb he was about to drop. Dan admitted that as crazy as it all sounded, there was obviously something to it, regardless of how unexplainable it was.

So then Christian gulped, took a deep breath, and started with the night his otherworldly visitor explained who he was, and showed what happened to him. As he was getting to the part where he recognized his grandfather getting out of his truck and walking towards Andrew, Dan groaned and put his head in his hands for several moments. When he finally looked up his eyes were filled with tears and he dabbed them away with a handkerchief. Half-sobbing he said, "That was the worst day of my life. I didn't mean for it to go that way. I was just trying to protect my daughter from being abandoned by some little shit that got her in trouble."

Christian said "Grandpa... I understand... I know it wasn't your intention to kill him. You got angry and things went bad." Christian then continued "But the major issue is that there's a guy who's innocent who's been in prison for eighteen years."

"Don't think that didn't torture me... to see someone else take the blame when I could have stepped forward," Dan said. "But if I stepped up and admitted it, my life would have been over. I had lived a perfectly clean life and I would have spent the rest of it in prison." He continued "Can you imagine the embarrassment it would have been to my family and friends? Remember, your grandmother had become disabled at that point. Who was going to take care of her the way I did?"

"But how much did you think about the guy who was blamed for it?" Christian asked. Dan explained "Well... I know this is going to sound terrible ...the stories that came out in the paper about that guy... he had a criminal history and had already served time in prison. I convinced myself that this guy was probably going to end up in prison again for something else. Maybe it was better having a guy like that off the streets." He concluded, "I know that's an awful way to look at it... but it's what I had to do to justify to myself for not coming forward and admitting it. Don't think I haven't thought about this thousands of times."

Christian assured him that he had not told anyone of his grandfather's involvement.

"Well," said Dan, "although technically I may not deserve it, I'm hoping we can keep it that way. I'm almost seventy years old, and the idea of dying in prison and leaving your grandmother alone is almost too much to bear."

Dan added, "When your mother met and later married Bryan and he immediately adopted you. I knew at least that you would have a wonderful father figure in your life."

"Yes," responded Christian. "He surely has been that, and I re-assured him that I would always consider him my dad."

"But," Christian cautioned, "I want you to know that I am going to try my best to see if I can help get this guy released from prison... but I'll do so without implicating you."

"Well, I can't ask for much more than that," Dan replied.

The two hugged and Christian walked out.

16

SPENDING AN INORDINATE amount of time and energy on his quest to exonerate Mr. Pinto, Christian felt it was beginning to consume his every waking moment. Even at work, conducting his various duties on various cars and dealing with customers, he found it difficult to focus. He knew he needed to get back to his other pursuits, continuing to perfect his technique on the cello, and improving his golf game. Now that he was finished with his high school band, he decided to sign up for lessons with a master cello player to help get him to the point where he could feel competent to audition for an orchestra. He wanted to make Mason Harrington proud. And he also began taking lessons from a local golf pro and would start playing at least three times a week.

Christian also found that employing some of the techniques suggested by Dr. Wahlstrom seemed to help him ward off images and visions most of the time when they were intrusive. He did consciously decide however that he did not want to lose his ability, but only to have a little more control over when it occurred. He feared that what happened to him would turn him into a different person, and he was determined to maintain the qualities and the core of who he was before. Pursuing those passions and activities would keep him grounded and never let him forget who he was.

Three days after visiting his grandfather, he received a letter from the district attorney's office. He was given an appointment to speak to the D.A. the following Monday at 2 p.m. He would spend many hours over the next week trying to prepare himself. He knew that an eighteen-year-old trying to sell this admittedly wild, unconventional story would be met by skepticism from the county's top law enforcement official. Likely, he would only be interested in what could be proven in court. He knew he might only have fifteen minutes to make his case, and he had to make every minute count. He would arm himself with everything at his disposal and hope that it all added up to a case worth considering.

17

ON WEDNESDAY EVENING, with five days to go before his meeting with the D.A., he decided to act on his much-needed break from constantly thinking about it. He got to reflect about Mason Harrington and what a relief it had been for him to finally have insight and a sense of understanding about why he was the way he was. The feelings of alienation, being a misfit, a square peg in a round hole, an oddball—all were starting to fade away.

He pulled out his high school yearbook and started to re-read Mason's obituary that he had tucked in it a couple weeks back. It gave him a warm, familiar feeling, almost as if he was reading a complimentary piece about himself. He got to the paragraph that listed those Mason was survived by and saw that there was a brother Charles of Greenwich, Connecticut and a sister Dorothy of White Plains, New York. Christian wondered if either of these siblings might still be alive eighteen years later and proceeded to do a search on his computer.

He was in fact able to locate a Charles Harrington, 73 years-old, living in Greenwich. With a bit more searching he was able to find an address. Now he had to think long and hard about the possibility of contacting him. How would such a meeting go?

After thinking about for a couple days, he made the bold decision to take a ride to Greenwich and knock on Charles' door.

The following Sunday morning, he decided to chance it and take the two-hour drive down to Greenwich. His GPS directed him to Charles' street and at just before two o'clock, he parked the Maserati his father let him drive in front of the large white beautifully maintained old colonial home. Before he got out of the car, he said out loud "Please Mason.... be with me." He then took the long walk up the cobblestone walkway and took a deep breath and rang the bell.

A distinguished looking man who appeared to be in his seventies answered the door and said, "Can I help you young man?"

Very nervously, Christian started. "Sir... Are you Charles Harrington?"

"Yes. That's me," he answered with a quizzical tone.

"I came here to talk about your brother Mason" Christian answered. "I have a very special connection to him that I'd like to share with you," he continued. "It's all very positive, and I think you'll find it quite fascinating."

Charles then said, "You seem much too young to have known him... but you also seem like a nice, polite young man, so why don't you come inside and tell me your story."

He continued "I miss my brother very much...and I like the thought of talking about him. It's been a while."

Once they were seated in the immaculate living room that featured antiques from wall to wall, Christian said "It's a bit of a long story, but I have to start from the beginning." He then told Mr. Harrington about being struck by lightning and spending a week in a coma. He tried to quickly go through the strange happenings that were occurring to him after, and the diagnosis agreed upon by neurologists. He spoke of the paranormal visits from his unknown biological father and things that he learned from him that were substantiated by his mother.

Then it came time to reveal the shocking reason for him coming to Mr. Harrington's home. "So," Christian continued cautiously, "my unexplainable ability to both see the future and to communicate with people who had passed was beyond dispute."

He tried to let that sink in for a moment to see if there was any reaction.

"Well," said Charles, "I guess I am in no position to dispute it. Life can be full of things that seem impossible to explain." He then asked, "So where does my brother fit into this?"

Christian looked down at the floor for several seconds then looked Charles in the eyes and began.

"A couple of weeks ago I had a visit from a man who was dressed in a black tuxedo. He had blond hair and a very close-trimmed beard. He identified himself as Mason Harrington. Charles looked at him with a stunned expression, mouth agape. "This is getting stranger by the moment" he exclaimed." He then got up and walked over to the mantel and took a framed photo down and brought it over to show his guest. It appeared to be a family photo that included five people. Looking at it, Christian shouted excitedly, "That's him.... that's Mason!" pointing to the man second from the right.

Charles responded, "Well, young man... I'm not sure how you would be so sure of that, but you are correct." Christian continued, "So he spoke to me that night. He said he left too soon, and he missed it here. He said that he found me and was able to continue on."

He then relayed to Charles that he was so curious about this mysterious man and why he would visit him, he started to do research on him to find out what he could.

"So, I happened to come across his obituary. I saw that he died four months before I was born." Christian continued. "Reading it, I was stunned to find the undeniable similarities between Mason and myself. It was all there... he played the cello... he loved to golf... he enjoyed coin collecting ... he loved antique foreign automobiles. These things have all been the passions of my life." He let that all sink in for a moment.

Christian then said, "Between what he said to me and what I learned... I have concluded that I was reincarnated from him."

All Charles could do was shake his head. After a moment he said, "Excuse me for a minute. I want to show you something."

After a couple of minutes, Charles walked back into the room carrying a cello and a bow. He said, "This was the cello that Mason used for most of his professional career. Would you like to play it?" Christian was in awe seeing the instrument. He also actually wondered if maybe Charles was testing him a bit to see if he really was a cello player. As he was handed the instrument, he sat in a different chair a few feet away, placed it properly between his legs, and ran the bow across each string a few times. Seeing that it was slightly out of tune, he adjusted the tuning keys until it was just right. When it was set, he started to slowly glide the bow across the strings and began playing a piece from Bach.

When he was done, Charles said, "That was utterly beautiful... and what you may not know is that it was one of Mason's favorite pieces. I heard him play it dozens of times."

"Well," replied Christian, "given what I believe in my heart, I guess it shouldn't surprise me. It was part of me."

Glancing back at the family photo, Christian then looked directly at Charles and said, "He's here with us right now. He's applauding... and he also wants me to tell you that he's pleased that you kept the family home."

"It was left to me by my mother... and given all our family history here ... I simply couldn't part with it, so I moved back in," said Charles.

Christian then said, "He wants us to go upstairs to his old room."

"Well... okay," said Charles. "At this point, I would probably do anything you asked me to do." He told Christian to follow him, as they went through a hallway and up a long staircase. Once on the second floor, they walked down the hallway and entered the second door on the right. "This was Mason's bedroom from the time he was very small until he left for college," said Charles.

"He's telling me to go to the three drawers that are built

into the wall," said Christian. "He wants you to open the bottom drawer and pull it all the way out." Charles followed these instructions, bending down and gradually removing the drawer completely. Christian then said. "He's telling you to reach inside the right side with your left hand... you will find something."

Charles bent down on his knees, reached in, and said, "Oh... there's something in here." He pulled out what looked like a small black tin lunch box with a small handle. He set it on a nearby desk and proceeded to open it. Inside was a large blue velvet cloth with something wrapped in it. Charles began to slowly unwrap the cloth to expose what appeared to be many dozens of silver coins, each wrapped in its own clear plastic casing. He picked one up and inspected it closely and said, "It's a 1964 John F. Kennedy half-dollar, apparently uncirculated" He started picking through the rest and found that they were all exactly the same. Tears welled up in his eyes as he said "When these were first issued in 1964, Mason was obsessed with collecting them. He was about fifteen at the time." He added, "I guess he found a little hiding spot for them and later forgot about it."

Charles started to count how many there were, and when he was done, he said to Christian "There are eighty-two of them, here."

Christian did a quick search on his phone and said, "This entire collection is worth a few thousand dollars." Charles replied, "And I never would have known about them if it wasn't for you." He then counted out ten of them and handed them to Christian and said "I want you to have these. I think Mason would approve, considering all we know now."

Christian thanked him profusely and then said, "He's telling me to tell you 'Good move Chuckles'"

"Oh my God," replied Charles, "I haven't heard that in years. He gave me that nickname when we were kids. It was his funny little version of Chuck," shaking his head and smiling.

After a moment, Charles said, "Let's go back downstairs. I have a couple other things I'd like to show you."

He asked Christian to follow him down to the basement. When they got down there, Charles went over to a corner where various items were stored and pulled out a large black golf club bag full of clubs. "These were the last set of clubs Mason used for the final few years of his life," said Charles. "He had a chance to golf with baseball pitching great Tom Seaver once and actually got the only hole-in-one of his life that day."

With Charles's approval, Christian took one of the clubs out of the bag and gripped it, saying "These are really fine professional quality clubs."

"Oh yeah," said Charles, smiling. "Nothing but the best for Mason." Charles then pulled the putter out of the bag and said "I'd like you to have this. I think he'd be okay with that, too."

"I will treasure it always, and I will use it. I think it will bring me good luck," He replied.

"There's one more thing I think you might appreciate. Come on out to the carriage house," said Charles. Once inside, Charles switched the light on and walked over to a vehicle parked in the corner and started to remove the large nylon cover. Once it was completely unveiled, Christian's jaw dropped. What he saw before him was an antique champagne-colored Mercedes-Benz sedan in extremely fine condition. "When it came to automobiles," said Charles, "this was his pride and joy. It's a 1978 model 600." Christian told him that he had seen one very similar at his father's dealership about two years before and instantly fell in love with it.

Back in the living room he noticed looking at the seven-foot-tall grandfather clock that it was nearly 3:30. He realized he had a long drive back home and told Charles he had to be leaving soon. Charles then said, "Before you go, give me a couple minutes... I've got one more thing." He excused himself and went into another room.

A few minutes later, he returned and handed Christian a very small fancy looking ceramic container with a small cover that was secured with a latch. "I have Mason's ashes in an urn, and I put some of them in here for you to keep."

"That is very kind" said Christian, "and I will keep them in a safe place."

As Christian was about to depart, Charles said to him, "This has been one of the most memorable, miraculous days of my life, and if I live to be one hundred and ten, I'll never forget it."

"Neither will I," Christian answered. "And I hope it's a comfort to know that in his own way, Mason will always be around."

"I will cling to that belief," said Charles. The two men hugged and said goodbye.

On the long drive up Route 95, Christian kept replaying the entire visit in his mind.

He would continue to pursue his passions, knowing now beyond any doubt where they came from.

18

MONDAY CAME AND Christian was mentally preparing for his meeting with Newport County District Attorney Adam O'Malley. He was going over and over his notes, rehearsing what he might say, and trying to anticipate questions he may be asked. He knew that he would likely only have one chance to make his case on behalf of Willy Pinto, and he had to be sharp and convincing.

He arrived at the office fifteen minutes ahead of his two o'clock appointment, checked in with the secretary, and sat in the waiting room. Looking at various plaques on the wall regarding previous district attorneys, he saw that this current D.A. was not in office at the time Pinto was charged and found guilty. Perhaps that might be something slightly in Pinto's favor. The current administration might not be as defensive to a mistake made by the previous one and may be more likely to overturn it. Christian proceeded to look over his notes, and finally a little after two, the secretary told him the D.A. would see him now. He thought to himself "Be sharp."

They introduced themselves, and Christian was directed to a chair right in front of the D.A.'s large desk. O'Malley then said, "So tell me how you became interested in Mr. Pinto's case."

"Well" said Christian, "It's a pretty long, involved, and very unusual story, but I'll do the best I can to sum it up." He started by explaining about being struck by lightning a couple months earlier, and O'Malley interjected that he remembered seeing that incident reported on the news. He then talked about his week-long coma, finally coming out of it, and several of the strange things that began to occur. He said that neurologists diagnosed him with the extremely rare Acquired Savant Syndrome and then handed O'Malley the doctor's letter confirming the findings.

The D.A. read it over and said, "Well... It appears that you are among a very select group of people."

Christian responded, "It's given me the ability to do and see things I never would have dreamed of. And that leads me to how I believe I know what I know about the death of Andrew Van Buren." He continued, "Along with seeing things that are going to happen in the future, I get visits from people who have passed. One person who visited me a few times was Andrew, and I came to learn from him that he is my biological father."

"This is all quite fascinating" said O'Malley, "but looking forward, I have to caution you that it's going to be a difficult thing to prove in a legal setting.'

"I do understand that" responded Christian. But when you hear what I saw, I think it makes it easier to believe. In his last visit, Andrew was able to show me in exact, explicit detail how it all occurred, from beginning to end. It was just like watching a movie."

"And you're absolutely certain this wasn't a dream?" asked the D.A.

"Well... I think when you hear about what I was able to see, it may be difficult to dispute. What he showed me was just like being a witness to the actual incident."

"So, give me the important details," said the D.A.

"Well," Christian began, I saw Andrew coming out of the restaurant to go to his car, and an older man came up and started hollering at him. He then punched Andrew... started hollering some more and punched him again. The second punch sent him to the ground, where it appeared he hit his head hard."

"And do you know who that man was?" O'Malley asked. Christian hated the idea of not being truthful, but feeling that he had to protect his grandfather, he simply said "No,"

"So then?" pushed O'Malley.

"About a half-minute later, a guy came walking through the parking lot. He saw Andrew lying there... looked around for a few seconds... and reached down and pulled the wallet out of his pants pocket. A few seconds later, a police car drove by slowly and stopped to investigate."

Christian concluded, "A minute or so later they placed him under arrest. This was the beginning of Willy Pinto's long nightmare."

"That's truly very interesting, and quite an example of the abilities you seem to have," said O'Malley. "But I'm not sure what I can do with it."

"Well," Christian then said, "Here's something that I observed that may appear to be a very small detail... but it may provide you with a piece of evidence that will make my vision completely legitimate." He sat forward in his chair and pulled a piece of paper out of his folder. "When I saw in the vision that Andrew was lying on the ground bleeding profusely, I happened to notice a car parked very near him. It was a dark green Subaru wagon with a Rhode Island license plate that read GC-3091. I'm sure the registry of motor vehicles has records going back several years and you could check who owned that car."

The D.A. started writing this information on a legal pad of paper and said, "Well I must admit," O'Malley exclaimed, "that is a pretty specific piece of evidence."

Christian continued, "If the owner of that car is still around, you could question them. If they were at that restaurant the night a murder was committed there, there's a good chance they would remember having been there. That would show that what I saw was accurate."

"I would say you've made a pretty interesting case at the very least," O'Malley said, "and you've given us something to follow up on."

Christian then said, "I'd like to add one thing before I leave."

"Sure, go ahead," said O'Malley.

"It is my understanding of the United States judicial

system," Christian said, "that the general principle is that they would much rather let a guilty person go free than find an innocent person guilty and incarcerate them. It seems that this would apply in this case."

O'Malley replied, "That's a pretty astute observation... a concept that I think gets overlooked quite often."

"There is one other thing I'd like to add," said Christian. Mediums and psychics have been used by law enforcement agencies all over the country to help solve crimes. I've read about a woman in New Jersey who was used on thousands of cases, and a woman in Maryland on many hundreds. There is a precedent for this type of thing."

District Attorney O'Malley arose from his desk and said, "I must say Mr. Casey... you've made an impassioned plea and you've got all your ducks in a row, so to speak. I will look into the matter and be in touch." With that they shook hands and Christian left the office.

On his drive home, Christian felt like he had represented his case well, but for the time being, it was largely out of his hands.

19

THAT EVENING CHRISTIAN wrote a letter to Willy telling him of his visit with the district attorney. He told him how he tried to make his best case and provided Willy with a few of the specific points he had made.

About a week later he received a letter back from Willy thanking him for all he was trying to do. He still said that he was trying not to get his hopes up too high, but that it was surely worth pursuing. Willy told Christian that he would be eligible for parole for the first time in about a year and a half, and that at the very least, maybe the D.A. could encourage them to rule in his favor at the parole hearing. Willy closed by saying "Man, for a kid just out of high school, you are a force of nature!"

A few days after that, Christian received a phone call from D.A. O'Malley, requesting that he come to his office that Friday morning at 10 o'clock. Christian was very hopeful that this indicated some progress.

He arrived at the office at the designated time and was called right in. The D.A. said to him "I might have at least *some* positive news for you." O'Malley went on to explain that they managed to track down the person who owned the automobile with the exact license plate Christian had seen in his vision. He was a middle-aged man now living in Warren, Rhode Island, and he was called in to the D.A.'s office the day before to answer questions. As it turned out, he was a cook at the restaurant that night, knew Andrew and distinctly remembered the murder occurring.

"So," O'Malley said, "however strange and bizarre this all seems, your vision appears to have been accurate." He then got up from his desk and walked around it and sat on the edge and looked Christian directly in the eyes and said "The problem is.... I just don't know how realistic it is to re-open this case. I don't see how it could be admitted as evidence. It's so unorthodox and unprecedented."

Showing his disappointment Christian said, "Is there any other option?"

The D.A. responded, "I would say the only thing I might consider at this point is kicking it up to the governor to see what his thoughts might be."

Christian then stated, "Mr. Pinto told me he is up for parole for the first time in about a year and a half. Is it possible that you might have some influence with the parole board?"

"Well," replied O'Malley, "we would have to see who is on the board at that particular time. I couldn't really speculate about that at this time."

He concluded "The best option I have right now is to turn this over to the governor and we'll just have to see how he views this."

Christian thanked him and left the office.

20

A COUPLE DAYS later, Christian received a letter from Dr. Woodward, the first neurologist who had suggested the diagnosis of Acquired Savant Syndrome. As he had suggested while Christian was still in the hospital, he wanted to start work on an article that would be a case history and a follow-up of his rare condition for a medical journal. He was requesting that Christian come to his office in Warwick sometime in the next couple of weeks so he could interview him at length about all that he had experienced.

Christian was flattered and felt that this would be his contribution to the medical world. His only request was that the doctor not reveal his real name.

By late July, Christian received a letter from Mark Blanchard, the governor of the state of Rhode Island. He requested that he come to his office at the state house in Providence the following week to discuss the Pinto case. As instructed, he called the governor's secretary to confirm the appointment. He chose to see a glimmer of hope in the situation, because he didn't think the governor would ask him to make the trip to his office to simply tell him he had no interest in the possibility of releasing Pinto.

Christian now threw himself into focusing on what he could do to make his presentation stronger. Lying awake one night, he saw a vision of Willy walking through the service area of his father's auto dealership, and it struck him. After his release, he believed he saw that Willy would be employed by Bryan in some capacity, but he knew that it was he who was going to have to initiate the idea.

He sat down with his father the following day and explained in full detail his vision of Andrew's death. He did so without revealing that he knew who it was that caused it, only that Willy happened to be in the wrong place at the wrong time.

He told Bryan of his efforts to have Pinto released, admitting that it might be a long shot. Speaking of his upcoming visit with the governor, he asked if there was a possibility that they could hire him at the dealership for a variety of tasks. Now that Christian was working full time and learning and training on several aspects of the business he had not been engaged in before, perhaps Willy could take over many of those duties. Christian had less time to clean and recondition cars, run to get auto parts, or assist the mechanics or sales associates in any way he could. If Christian could convince the governor that Willy had a job waiting for him upon his release, that might be something in his favor.

Bryan agreed to this possibility.

Christian was beginning to feel more confident about his trip to the state house.

21

THE MORNING OF his appointment with the governor finally arrived. Christian parked his vehicle just a short way down the hill and walked up to the impressive, historic old building that had served the state for 125 years. Walking up the steps he remembered coming here on a school field trip in the ninth grade. He had never imagined that less than four years later he would have business here and be sitting in the governor's office having a one-on-one conversation with him.

After going through the usual security procedures with a state police officer, Christian was allowed to enter the room where the Governor's secretary sat at her desk. After giving her his name, she picked up the telephone and said, "Mr. Casey is here." A moment later the door swung open and out walked Governor Blanchard, whom Christian only recognized from seeing him on television. He felt a bit like a VIP when the governor said, "Mr. Casey come right in... I've been looking forward to speaking with you."

Once seated in front of the desk, Gov. Blanchard stated, "I was quite fascinated with what District Attorney O'Malley told me about this, but I really wanted to hear it all directly from you." First off, in your own words, tell me how you came to have this ability you seem to have."

Christian started with the lightning strike and went through the progression of events of the following months. He tried to keep his story very consistent with the way he told it to D.A. O'Malley. At that point the governor's phone rang and he said, "Please excuse me for just a moment... I have to take this call,but I'll be very brief."

While the governor was on the phone, Christian happened to notice an autographed baseball in a clear plastic container sitting on the desk just a couple of feet away. He stared at it for a moment, and when the governor hung up the phone and started to apologize, Christian said "Your Uncle Walter is pleased you still display this ball. He remembers taking you down to a game at Yankee Stadium when you were a kid where you got a few players to sign this ball. He's smiling."

"Oh my God!" the governor exclaimed with a shocked look on his face. "You can see that?" He added, "I can't believe you're performing your magic right in front of me. You are the real deal, son."

"Well sir, if I may," responded Christian, "I am hopeful that you will see that the car and the license plate that I saw in my vision—which turned out to be proven to have actually been there that night, will help to validate that what I saw was accurate."

"Well," the governor replied, "there doesn't appear to be

any other logical explanation for it, and I am certainly inclined to believe that things happen that are beyond our comprehension. "But proving something in a court of law is quite a bit different. That's what could be problematic in this particular case."

"There's one other thing," Christian remembered, "that I know you might be concerned about when releasing an inmate that's been locked up for nearly nineteen years. Where's he going to live and what's he going to do for work? I think we've got that covered." Christian explained that his father would give Willy a job at his auto dealership, and that he also owns a small apartment complex that has a vacant studio unit that he could rent to him for a very reasonable price.

Christian then geared himself up to go for it all. "Sir," Christian began, "I am in absolutely no position to tell you how to govern... but it is my understanding that you have it within your authority to commute a prison sentence. You can forego the district attorney and the courts, and I don't believe you even need to explain."

Set to make his final plea, Christian concluded, "If due to my gift—which I can take no credit for—you accept that Willy Pinto was just in the wrong place at the wrong time and has served nearly nineteen years for a crime he did not commit, then releasing him at this point seems like the proper thing to do."

"I must say Christian.... you seem wise far beyond your years... and you make a very impassioned, compelling case." He then pivoted to a more self-serving thought, asking Christian,

"I am very impressed and I think I could use someone like you on my re-election campaign. Would you consider it?"

"Give me one minute," Christian said. He then held up his index finger, as if asking for a pause, stared the governor in the eyes for about ten seconds, then closed his eyes for a few moments.

When he opened his eyes back up, he said to the governor, "I see you giving your winning acceptance speech next election night. You don't need my help."

Shaking his head, the Governor said, "You have to be one of the most amazing people I've ever spoken to." As he rose from his desk, he said, "I'm going to give serious consideration to your suggestion, and I will contact you when I come to a decision."

Christian left feeling he had made the best impression he possibly could have.

22

IT SEEMED LIKE a good time to go back to the correctional facility Willy was housed at and catch him up with all that had occurred regarding his case. Christian went the evening after his trip to the state house, and this time at least knew what to expect regarding what he had to go through to get to the visiting room. When Willy finally came in and sat down, Christian said, "Well my friend, I've got quite a bit to report."

"Geez man... this is like a TV show that keeps you hanging with twists and turns," laughed Willy.

"Well," said Christian, "I've met with both the D.A. and the damn governor of the state, and I've got to tell you... I think they're really thinking about it." He said excitedly. He continued, "And while their big concern is that this is the kind of thing that is impossible to prove in court, as you had said when we first met, I tried to convince the governor that commuting your sentence was a legitimate alternative."

"Well, that's an angle I hadn't really thought of," Willy replied.

Christian added, "It's a decision he can basically make all on his own without involving the D.A. or the courts. And when I was able to display some of my gift right in front of him, I think it gave my story credibility."

Christian then told Willy about his offer of working at the dealership and the availability of a small apartment nearby where he could live, and how it would strengthen the case for his release. "Jesus," exclaimed Willy, "you've got all the bases covered."

"The other thing I have to tell you," Christian said 'was that I had a brief vision last night of you sitting at a table across from the governor talking to him. So, I think it's very likely that he's going to come here to speak to you."

"Wow," said Willy, "I guess I'm really going to have to make a really good first impression."

"Well," Christian replied, "I think you should make it a point to say you made a terrible mistake in lifting Andrew's wallet that night and maybe putting yourself in a position to appear guilty, but stress that it was the only thing you did wrong."

"Well," said Willy, "I can look him in the eye and say that and know that I'm telling the truth."

Christian added, "I think that's very important. Look him in the eye when speaking to him. He'll sense your sincerity, like I do."

"It would also be good to tell him about your cellmate of several years back who really helped change your outlook and your attitude. And that you're very much looking forward to the possibility of working at our dealership and returning to a decent, productive life."

Willy then said, "If we're successful at this, I just don't know any way I could ever make it up to you."

Christian said, "My father Andrew told me right from the beginning that I had been given a wonderful gift... and to use it wisely. This is what it's for."

23

FIVE DAYS LATER a dark sedan with official state license plates pulled up to the front of the Adult Correctional Institution. Out of the automobile emerged the commissioner of the department of corrections and Governor Blanchard. They were there to meet with institution's superintendent and the medical director regarding several issues and new policies, and to tour the facility. The governor was also going to set aside time for a brief meeting with Willy Pinto.

After the conclusion of all the other business that needed attention, the governor instructed the superintendent to have Willy escorted by the director of security and an assistant deputy superintendent to a small, out of the way office near the administrative wing. Governor Blanchard wanted as few people as possible to know what was going on regarding Pinto. He knew that if the inmate was escorted by correction officers who worked on the blocks and they got wind of what was going on, it would be spread throughout the prison within an hour.

With the two men on either side of him, Willy was brought into the small room and told to be seated at a table. A couple moments later, the governor entered the room, nodded at the two officials, and introduced himself to Willy.

Governor Blanchard sat at the table across from Willy and began, "Mr. Pinto, I've been reviewing your case recently since information has surfaced that calls into question your guilty verdict in 2008. I'd like you to take me back to the incident for which you were arrested, and in your own words, tell me the whole story."

Willy cleared his throat, took a deep breath, and began to tell the story. He was emphatic that it was due to his dire financial situation that he saw the opportunity to help himself to whatever money might be in man's wallet. "It was absolutely stupid of me," Willy said, "and I've been sorry about it every day since it happened. It was a terrible decision, and I put myself in a position to be blamed for the young man's death."

"And you've been visited by Christian Casey a couple of times, I see," said the governor. "Yes... he's really a remarkable young man. I think he was sent to me from above."

"He certainly is like no one else I've ever met", responded the governor.

"Now tell me Mr. Pinto," he continued. "If by chance a decision went your way and you are released, tell what your plans would be."

"Christian told me that his father will hire me to work at their car dealership, and that there is a small studio apartment that I could rent. After what I've been through, I'd consider myself extremely lucky to start a new life.... And I promise I will not blow it."

"Well, that's good to hear," the governor replied. "It sounds like you have a good attitude.

Willy interjected, "Well, I had a cellmate several years back that really helped reshape my way of thinking, and it really gave me a whole new outlook".

"I guess it's like with young Mr. Casey," the governor added. "Sometimes you just never know when good things are going to come your way."

As the governor rose from his chair, he said, "Try to be patient Mr. Pinto. I'm going to give this a lot of thought." He shook Willy's hand and left the room. The two correction officials then escorted him back to his block. He felt good about the conversation and continued to replay it in his mind for hours. He did not speak of what had just transpired to any of his fellow inmates.

Now all he could do was wait.

24

ONE EVENING AFTER dinner, Bryan had stepped out to do a couple of errands, and Christian sat down in the living room to talk to his mother. Something had occurred to him that he had to ask about. He started, "Mum, whatever happened to Andrew's parents? They're technically my grandparents. Where they ever part of my life early on?"

"No," she said. "I hate to say it, but they never bothered with us. I heard that they moved to Florida a little while after Andrew died, and that's the last I ever heard about them."

He then asked, "Was Andrew buried around here, or was he cremated?"

"No, he's buried at a cemetery in Middletown. I visited the grave a few times way back, but it's been many, many years." She then recalled, "I actually took you there once when you were about a year old."

"Tell me the name of the cemetery if you can remember." he said. "I think I'd like to go there at least once."

A few days later, Christian drove to the next town over and drove through the large granite entrance of Columbus Cemetery and followed the directions as his mother had vaguely remembered them. Believing he was in the general area he parked his car and started walking, scanning the rows of gravestones. He finally spotted the name Van Buren on a stone about fifty feet away.

Christian walked up close to it and read the inscription. *Andrew J. Van Buren 1988 – 2007 Forever in Our Hearts.*

He could picture so clearly how Andrew looked in his three visions. It was a face he would never forget. He got down on one knee and pondered what little he actually knew about him. As he was deep in thought he heard a woman's voice from behind him, and he turned around to see a lady appearing to be in her mid-forties. She had said, "I've never seen you here before... were you acquainted with Andrew? You seem a little too young to have known him."

Christian paused for a moment and then answered, "Well Ma'am... we do have a certain connection... but it's a really long, strange story."

She said "I'm Andrew's older sister Melanie. I wouldn't mind hearing your story."

Pointing over to a nearby bench, Christian said, "Maybe we should sit down. This gets pretty involved." Once seated he introduced himself and then slowly started from the beginning.

Once she heard about the lightning strike she said, "I did happen to see that on the news a few months ago... that was you?" He then continued his story and took a pause before he got to Andrew's visit.

As he started to relay that aspect, Melanie's eyes grew very wide, and she had an astonished look on her face. As if on cue, Christian could see Andrew standing a few feet away, telling him to call her "Lemanie." It was almost as if Andrew knew that this would help to convince her that what he was saying was all true. Following those instructions, Christian said to her, "He's here with us now... and he's telling me to call you 'Lemanie'."

"Oh, my goodness!" she cried. "That's what he first called me when he was a toddler because he couldn't pronounce 'Melanie'. To him... I was Lemanie... and it stuck. Later, he shortened it to Lem." With tears in her eyes, she said, "You would have no possible way of knowing any such thing. I have to believe what you're saying is somehow true." She added "you actually feel him here now?"

"Yes... and he's still wearing his waiter's uniform." She looked up and whispered, "I love you, Andrew."

"Well," Christian said, "there's a lot more. He then revealed the second visit, and then the crucial third visit in which he was able to show Christian how he was killed. Describing the events of that night got Melanie sobbing, never hearing these specific details at the trial because there were no witnesses. He then got to the part that revealed that Willy Pinto was not the killer, and she was utterly stunned. Continuing to protect his grandfather, Christian made it clear that he couldn't tell who the real perpetrator was but repeated that he knew it wasn't Pinto. He was emphatic that based on his vision, it was the right thing to do to attempt to get him released from a sentence for a crime he did not commit.

Melanie begrudgingly admitted that he was right about that but wondered how her parents might feel.

Christian then asked, "My mother tells me that they never really had anything to do with me after I was born. Do you know why?"

"Well," said Melanie, "I think they were not happy that none of your family came to the trial for support. That's what I seem to remember. Then they thought that they heard you were given up for adoption. Shortly after that they felt the need to get away and moved to Florida."

"The fact is," Christian said, "my mother started dating another guy a couple months before I was born, and he adopted me very shortly after. My mother never gave me up." He added "I grew up believing that Bryan Casey was my biological father, and I never knew until it was revealed to me by Andrew that it was really him."

"This is like a movie," Melanie remarked. "So, I guess you've already figured out that I'm your aunt?" said Melanie. "Yes" smiled Christian, "I guess we both just discovered a new relative."

"So, Melanie... I mean... *Aunt Melanie*... can you tell me a little bit about my father?"

"I will tell you," she said, "he was a really sharp, smart kid. He was on his way to the University of Pennsylvania. I honestly think he would have ended up going to law school. He loved to debate, and when he thought he was right, he would argue endlessly until he thought he had you convinced." She continued, "When he was really interested in something, he became very fixated... almost obsessed... and he was very determined to succeed."

"I will say," said Christian, "I might have gotten those traits from him. When I really get into something, I give it my all."

"Well," she said, "it's nice to know that a little bit of him lives on.... And I will tell you... you actually do resemble him a little bit."

Christian then asked, "Would you happen to have a photo of him that you would consider parting with?"

She replied, "Give me your address, and I'll find one and mail it to you."

She then said, "If you are successful at getting that man released from prison, I think I might not tell my parents about it. It would only bring back that old terrible pain and make them realize that the real killer went unpunished." Christian replied, "I can completely understand that."

The two then hugged and said goodbye.

25

ARRIVING HOME FROM the cemetery, Christian saw that he had a letter from Willy. In it he told all about his meeting with the governor, and that he felt it went very well. While he got a good feeling and felt Governor Blanchard really listened to him, he still had a basic mistrust of politicians in general and was still trying very hard not to get his hopes up. Christian jotted out a brief letter acknowledging that he received it, that he had a good feeling about the situation, and that he would be in touch soon.

Three days later, Christian received a phone call directly from the governor asking if he and his father could come to his office On Thursday morning at 11:30. He responded that he would have to check with his father and that he would leave a message with the governor's secretary as soon as possible.

Bryan was able to agree to the meeting and gave the okay. He knew this project meant a lot to Christian and was proud that he would take such a proactive role in doing what he felt was right.

Thursday morning came and the Caseys went to the state house in Providence, and after waiting briefly, they entered the governor's office at the scheduled time. They were greeted warmly by Governor Blanchard who sad to Bryan, "I've never met anyone quite like this young man," gesturing to Christian. "Yes, he's his own man, and he can be pretty relentless," beamed Bryan.

After they were seated the governor began, "I want you to know that I'm strongly leaning towards a commutation for Mr. Pinto, but I'd like to make certain he is set up for his best chance of success. I need an assurance from you Mr. Casey that you will give him a job at your dealership upon release."

"Yes," answered Bryan. "Now that Christian is moving up and learning many more phases of the business, we could definitely use another person around."

The governor then asked, "And Christian had mentioned a small apartment where he could live?"

"Yes" Bryan replied. "I own an eight-unit apartment building in Middletown that has a vacant studio apartment, already semi-furnished. We have a few other items in our basement he would be welcome to." He then added, "We can have it all ready to go when he needs it."

"Well, that's exactly what I needed to hear," the governor assured them. He will be scheduled for release at nine o'clock on Monday morning. "If it's okay, we can have a state transportation van drop him off at your dealership." Both men nodded in agreement. They were then informed that a state-appointed social worker was going to check in on Willy each day for a while until he got acclimated to life on the outside. "And there is one other thing I'd like to ask," said the governor. "I'd like to keep this all as confidential as possible. I know how the media can be. If any of them come snooping around looking for a story or an interview, play dumb and don't tell them anything."

"For all you've done," said Bryan, "that's the least we can do."

On the ride home, Christian told his father that when in his vision Andrew told him to use his gift wisely, this is exactly the kind of thing he was talking about. At that moment, he thought he saw something out of the corner of his eye and turned to look in the back seat. Andrew was sitting there looking at Christian with his two thumbs up.

26

ON SATURDAY MORNING Christian went to the dealership for a few hours. He set out to clean up a 2017 BMW that had just been traded in for a late model Aston Martin. As he opened the trunk of the BMW, he began experiencing a very vivid vision. He saw what he somehow knew was a dead body wrapped up tightly in a dark brown heavy canvas tarp. He then saw two men lift the body out of the trunk and carry it over to a large hole in the ground and lower it into it. One of the men then grabbed a shovel lying near a pile of dirt and began shoveling the dirt into the hole.

Christian immediately realized that he should pay very close attention and pick up on every detail he could that might help identify where and when this occurred. Similar to the vision of Andrew's murder, he was able to spot the Rhode Island license plate on the back of the BMW and committed it to memory. He also recognized what appeared to be a portion of the Route 95 expressway overpass in the distance with a familiar landmark nearby. The vision began to fade as the makeshift grave was nearly filled.

Christian had to stop and sit down to fully digest what he had just experienced. He couldn't help but think that he was likely going to now be embroiled in another murder investigation. Should he contact the district attorney again to tell him he had clues for a different case?

He gathered all the paperwork pertaining to this particular automobile which included not only the year, model, official color and vehicle identification number, but previous owner. He also realized that there may have been more than one previous owner, and the question could become which one may have been part of the vision. He was going to have to give this a lot of thought before proceeding.

His father came around the corner and saw him deep in thought with a strange look on his face. Bryan said "Hey... you look like you've seen a ghost," and then realized in this case, that might not be too far off from what just happened.

"Dad... I had another experience... involving this car. Let's hold off on putting it out for sale for a while." Brian replied "Okay... we can do that."

Lying awake in bed that night, he thought maybe he could recapture the vision as he had done with Andrew's death. Try as he may, concentrating deeply, he just couldn't get himself there. He finally decided to set it aside for the time being and give it more thought, revisiting the idea in a couple days.

27

ON MONDAY MORNING, Christian was trying to keep busy around the dealership showroom, keeping an eye out for Willy's arrival. Finally, at about 10:45, he saw a gray state department of corrections van pull up and a man in a blue blazer got out of the driver's side. He came inside, asking for both Bryan and Christian to officially accept custody of Willy and sign a form. The transportation officer then went out to the van with the Caseys following behind and unlocked the back door as Willy proceeded to climb out.

With a big smile on his face, and his eyes a bit misty, he shook both of their hands and said to them "Gentlemen... this is the first day of my new life... and I have the both of you to thank. This is like a dream. I promise you will never be sorry."

Bryan said with a smile, "Welcome to your new job at International Motor Carriages."

Willy joked, "Boy... I've made a pretty big jump in one hour."

Christian added, "Well... let's try to put the past behind and move forward as best we can." He then gave Willy a detailed tour of the entire dealership, introduced him to all his new fellow employees, and tried to explain everything he would need to know.

Come lunchtime, Willy was having a sandwich in the employee break room and Christian said that he would be back in a few minutes. He grabbed the keys to the newly received BMW which he had the experience with and decided on a close-up approach to recapture his previous vision. He believed that maybe close contact might just trigger that all again.

He approached the vehicle, now parked in the lot behind the dealership, and walked very slowly around it, touching it as he stepped to try to pick up vibes as he was concentrating deeply. He got to the back and very slowly unlocked the trunk, raised the lid, took three slow steps backward, and closed his eyes for about ten seconds.

When he opened his eyes, there was the scene playing out again. This time, he would look for any small detail that might assist in identifying an approximate period of time and exact location where the body was buried.

Two small things on the back of the car jumped out at him. On the license plate was a tiny registration sticker that had the number "2019" on it that indicated it would expire at some point that year. There was also a small bumper sticker on the rear that had a New England Patriots football team logo with the words "Super Bowl LIII Champs."

He also maintained the presence of mind to scan the

landscape and seemed to believe it was an area in Providence just off interstate Route. 95 as he had suspected in his first vision.

As it started to fade, and he came back to the present, he began writing these details down. He now felt he might have enough information to possibly develop a theory as to when and where it occurred.

He went back inside and continued to be shadowed by Willy for the afternoon. At closing time, Christian gave him a ride to see his new apartment and the unlikely pair stopped and got a few groceries to hold Willy over for a few days. He was getting a tremendous kick out of being out in public and among people doing everyday normal things that he hadn't experienced in nearly two decades. When they arrived at the apartment and Christian unlocked the door, Willy stepped inside, dropped to his knees, and put his hands together as if to pray. Through tears he said, "I'm so afraid I'm going to wake up and be back in prison."

"I can assure you it's real," said Christian. "And you're still young and you've got a long, interesting life ahead of you."

"Bless you my friend" replied Willy.

That evening, Christian sat down to try to re-construct what he saw in the vision and to research a couple aspects of it to establish some of the important details. He looked at his notes and focused on the football bumper sticker. *Super Bowl LIII* referred to the 53rd championship game that he found was held on February 3, 2018. The bumper sticker was celebrating the victory in that game by the New England Patriots, which meant that it could not have been produced before that date.

The registration sticker on the license plate that read *2019* would indicate that the vehicle's registration would expire at least sometime before 2020. He also happened to observe that the two men who lifted the body out of the trunk were wearing long wool coats, so it would appear to be a cold weather month.

But the one small detail that might really narrow down a possible time frame was a very large billboard off the expressway that could be seen by oncoming traffic. It was an advertisement for an old-time popular 1990s rock band that would be coming to play a show at a gambling casino in Connecticut on March 15, 2018. In all likelihood, once that date had passed, the billboard would have been changed and another ad put up in its place. So, with these key pieces of evidence, Christian felt he could determine that the vision he saw would have occurred sometime between February 4th and March 15th of 2018.

He now felt confident that he was building a possible case that he could take to the District Attorney—but because the crime likely occurred in Providence, he would now have to deal with the D.A. of Providence County. He was not fond of the prospect of having to explain his entire story all over again about how he came to possess his abilities. He wondered if maybe he could contact D.A. O'Malley from Newport and ask him to give a reference to the Providence County D.A. to possibly give him a foot in the door.

For now, he would attempt to re-create all the information his vision provided, including possible time, place, and perpetrators. His father's dealership was in possession of the

vehicle, and as in the previous case, the registry of motor vehicles could identify exactly who owned it during the likely six-
week time frame of the crime. He planned to take a ride that
weekend along Route 95 in Providence to attempt to locate
the area where his vision occurred. He felt as though he had
seen enough of the surrounding landscape to possibly identify it, and this would be one of the most crucial aspects. He
would likely have to be able to direct the authorities to a spot
where a body could be searched for and ultimately exhumed.
From there, unsolved murders from that time and likely dental records would be required. Christian's new project was to
iron out all these details before he contacted the authorities.

28

DESPITE ALL HIS activity concerning Willy's release, and his latest vision, Christian still found time to pursue his passions. He had entered an amateur golf tournament to be held in early September, coincidentally at the golf course where he was struck in late April. It was extremely eerie for him to walk out to the first hole and think back to the life-changing incident. Taking a few practice swings before the match was set to begin, he looked to his right about twenty feet to a large, wooded area and saw the image of Mason Harrington, dressed in golf clothing. Looking directly at Christian, he said, "This is where it happened... the thing that allowed you and I to make our connection." Mason then gave him a thumbs up and slowly faded away.

Christian had the best day of his career as a golfer, and won the tournament by a good margin, using Mason's putter throughout the round.

He was also making wonderful progress on his cello, and

his private teacher encouraged him to audition for a local orchestra called the Narragansett Bay Symphony Community Orchestra. With an endorsement from the teacher, he was able to set up an audition for a couple weeks later. Christian was also told by his teacher that the orchestra that worked at a theater in Warwick needed a cello player for a one-time musical production that would be staged in a few weeks. He was hired for what would be his first experience in an actual orchestra pit. He was now a professional cello player. Mason again made a very brief appearance to him at the very beginning of the show.

Christian would lie awake in bed at night giving a lot of thought to the abilities that he possessed and why it was him that this unique situation was bestowed. Was it just an accident of fate, or was there some higher power that chose him for this? As much as he had tended to previously feel like an outsider and a loner even among his friends and peers, that feeling was heightened far more with his extremely unusual powers. Who could he even discuss it with who could understand and relate to it personally?

He began to search out the names of mediums and found that there was a bookstore/café/spa in nearby Bristol that occasionally featured mediums that would conduct events for large groups and also book one-on-one sessions. It was called "The Other Side," and he decided to take a ride there one evening. Looking around inside, he saw a few posters on the wall advertising psychics and mediums who would be appearing soon, as well as information on booking an individual session with them. Christian asked the clerk behind the counter if it would even be possible to speak to any of them very briefly any time soon. "Well... it's funny you should ask," the clerk said. The medium Noreen Churchill is here right now doing a private session." She then went over and pointed to her photo on one of the posters. "She's probably going to be done with her session soon. Possibly when she comes out she'd have a couple minutes for you if you care to wait."

"Yes... that would be great," replied Christian.

He was browsing around looking at various books on holistic wellness, spiritual topics, angels, life after death, life stories, and biographies of psychics and mediums when the clerk alerted him that Noreen had just emerged from the back room area. Christian approached her and introduced himself and asked for just a few moments of her time. "It's a really long story," he said to her, "but the bottom line is... I have been experiencing psychic and medium powers, and there isn't a person in the world I know that I can talk to about it who can relate to it at all." He concluded "I thought maybe someone like you might understand."

Observing what almost seemed like desperation in Christian's face and voice, Noreen said, "Why don't we go out and sit in one of the back rooms and talk."

He replied "Oh... I would appreciate that so much."

Seated in comfortable chairs facing each other, Christian spontaneously experienced a medium-like moment. He relayed this experience to Noreen, telling her, "There is a golden Labrador retriever standing beside you wagging its tail."

With an astonished look on her face, she said, "Well... I guess you've just proven your ability beyond any doubt. I lost

Blondie three years ago, and it's wonderful to know she's still around me."

"Yes," he replied, "as much as you miss her, I know there's some consolation to know that she is in that other dimension… but very close."

Christian went on to explain his whole story about how he came to possess his abilities. He provided many examples and told the story of Willy Pinto. When he also added the visions of various people's future, Noreen commented "I've known a few mediums and a few psychics… but I can't say I've known one that possessed both abilities. You would appear to be unique in that regard." She added "There are two other mediums and a psychic that appear here occasionally whom I'm very friendly with. I think they'd be very interested in meeting you and hearing your fascinating story. I think that would also satisfy your desire to be around people who can relate to what you experience."

"That would be a privilege," said Christian.

Noreen said, "I'll tell you what… The four of us get together once a month or so, and we're about due. Why don't we exchange contact information, and you can come over to my house in Warren when we get together within the next week or two."

Driving home, Christian really felt like he had made a great connection suddenly feeling less lonely and isolated.

29

CHRISTIAN DECIDED TO subscribe to a newspaper archives website so that he could research old editions of the *Providence
Journal* newspaper to see if he could locate stories from the
period in question about a missing person or unsolved death.
He had no way of knowing if the body he saw buried had
ever been located later on and exhumed, or if that aspect had
remained a mystery.

Scanning page after page for many hours, he finally came
upon a brief story in an edition from early March of 2018 that
reported that a 39-year-old Cranston man named Shane Tourino was reported missing by his brother. A photo of the man
was included, but there were no other details of significance.
Christian continued to search subsequent editions and only
found one follow-up story from a week later indicating that
the man was still missing. The thought occurred to him to
check one other resource. He would go to the Cranston City
Hall. He knew that at the clerk's office there would be a file

containing index cards of every person who died while a resident of the city.

There was no card, and the clerk told him that she remembered the incident and had heard that he was never found as far as she knew.

Christian decided to ask Willy to take a ride with him up Route 95 in the Providence area to see if he could locate the precise spot he saw in his vision. He convinced his father to allow him to put a set of dealer plates on the BMW involved in the crime, thinking that with it being at the scene he may be able to call up the vision one more time to help confirm the location. He knew that it was a slightly remote area just beneath the elevated portion of the expressway, with no buildings nearby, and could not be viewed by cars driving along the major route. They got off at a couple different exits but there was no familiarity, but the third exit they tried struck a chord with Christian. "This is it I think" he said to Willy. "There's the large billboard I saw. Let me see if I can find the spot that gives me the exact same angle of it that my vision showed me."

He parked the car in what he thought might be the right spot, then got out and walked ten feet behind it to check the angle. He saw that he had to move it a little to the left and up a few feet. Once he put it in a better position, he got out and came around to the back of the car and once again, like he did back at the dealership, opened the trunk, hoping to capture that vision just one more time. He walked back about fifteen feet behind the car and closed his eyes and concentrated deeply for about ten seconds. Willy was standing nearby watching it all in sheer amazement.

When he opened his eyes, the scene was miraculously play-ing out all over again. The two men, whom he could really only see from behind lifted the body out and carried it over to a hole about ten feet away, dropping it in.

Christian then opened his eyes, and everything seemed to line up... the position of the car in relation to the expressway above... the billboard, which now had an advertisement for Rolex watches... he was confident he was in the exact spot. At this time, he went to the car and grabbed a can of red spray paint and walked over to where he estimated the hole had been dug. He wanted to mark it for future reference in case a crew would be sent out to dig—but he didn't want to make it too obvious to some person wandering around the area in the next few weeks—such as a big red circle... or a big "X" that might prompt some curiosity seeker to think that something was buried here. He decided to spray four small red dots on the ground about the size of a tennis ball at the four corners of what would be about a ten-foot by ten-foot square. He was certain that skeletal remains would be found under there, and it would lead to a major step forward in the case. Before leav-ing, he took several photos of the area.

Christian now felt like he had all he needed to proceed. He finally wrote a letter that night to the Newport district attor-ney explaining that he had a recent vision that might lead to solving a murder that occurred several years before in Provi-dence. He simply asked if the D.A. could contact his counter-part in Providence County and explain that his abilities had helped with a previous case and that it was all a legitimate avenue to make progress on a cold case. Christian closed with the idea that he would wait to hear back from D.A. O'Malley before contacting the Providence office.

Later that night, in the wee hours of the morning, he awoke to find a vision of a man standing six feet away. Studying him for a moment, he recognized him from the photo of Shane Tourino in the missing persons article. Once the vision was fully clear, he spoke the words. "You found me... My family will thank you," before gradually fading away.

Christian knew he was over the target.

30

THE NEXT DAY Christian received a phone call from Noreen Churchill, telling him that he was invited to her house that Sunday to get together with her and the two other mediums and the psychic she had talked about.

Arriving at her house on the designated afternoon, she introduced him to a male medium named Noah Lazarus and Ophelia St. John, a female medium. The other lady was a psychic named Lilly Larsson. Christian initially felt a slight bit of awkwardness at the realization that they were all likely more than twice his age. The discomfort faded quickly as they all treated him very nicely and seemed very eager to hear his story. They were all quite amazed, none of them ever having met a person who had developed these types of abilities in this fashion or had personally known anyone with a diagnosis of Acquired Savant Syndrome. They also marveled at his dual abilities to both see the future and communicate with those who had passed. They actually made him feel very accepted and at ease.

Each had a chance to tell some of their more interesting, compelling stories of their individual experiences. The four, who had known each other for some time, tried to dig deep to recite stories that they had not told each other previously.

Christian finally had a chance to tell the entire story of Willy, and they all congratulated him on a wonderful use of his gift. They seemed somewhat envious of his ability to positively affect someone's life in such a profoundly positive way.

Lilly, who had written a book with a co-author about her psychic abilities and experiences, remarked that her fellow author might be interested in the possibility of writing a book about Willy's life story. Christian said, "That sounds like a very interesting idea—as long as they use a made-up name for me when discussing my role in his release. I'm not looking for a lot of attention," he said with a smile. He added, "The doctors warned us to keep a low profile about my abilities... And if it became public knowledge, I would be hounded by people constantly looking for sessions about their future and their deceased relatives."

Noreen replied, "Well... I think we can all relate to the idea of getting more requests for private readings than we can handle." The other three nodded in agreement.

Christian then said to Lilly, "I can tell you that I had a premonition about Willy that he was standing at a podium, talking to a crowd at some type of hall, and he was holding up a book. So, I think it's possible that me meeting you was part of the chain of events that was going to make that book happen."

"Bravo," said Ophelia, "you are an incredibly insightful young man..... wise beyond your years."

"Well," said Christian, "let me tell you my story about reincarnation and being an *old soul.*"

Lilly and Christian exchanged contact info and said that they would follow up on the idea of possibly hooking the author up with Willy about the concept of working on his life story.

Christian felt the afternoon with these folks was very therapeutic and he had not been in a social situation in which he had felt so accepted and at home in a very long time. He felt as if he was now a new member of a special fraternity and that these were people who truly understood and related to his situation.

It was the first time in quite a while that he did not feel like a freak.

31

THAT WEEK, CHRISTIAN received a phone call from the conductor of the Narragansett Bay Symphony Orchestra to see if he was interested in coming to their next rehearsal to audition for a spot. One of the cello players was going to be taking some time off in a couple of months and a spot would be open for a few performances. The conductor instructed him to arrive half an hour early, and if things went well, he could remain for the entire rehearsal. Christian was very excited and promised to be there.

Around that same time, he also received a phone call from Newport D. A. O'Malley informing him that he had a conversation with Providence County D.A. Nick Grasso about him, and that he should submit what information he has by letter as soon as possible. Christian then went to work putting together an outline to help organize his thoughts in order to write the best, most effective letter he could to convince the district attorney that he could help solve a murder mystery. He would provide information on the exact vehicle that was used, the location of the disposal of the body, and a fairly specific time frame. He would even have the photos of the area that he took printed out and include them. Everything would seem to be in order to possibly re-open the case. After working on it for a couple of days, he finally dropped it in the mail.

The day arrived for him to attend his audition, and he drove to a small auditorium in Warwick where it would take place. He met the conductor, and elderly man with a generous shock of white hair named Eric von Bauer. He greeted Christian and handed him several pieces of sheet music that would be the ultimate test of his ability.

Waving his baton, as he would during a performance to control the tempo, he put Christian through the paces and smiled on occasion, pleased with what he was hearing. After completing three pieces, von Bauer said with a smile, "Well young man... I think you're qualified to take your place as the youngest member of our orchestra. I'll show you where you'll be seated for our rehearsal tonight. Christian was thrilled and felt he had taken another big step in his blossoming music career.

Taking his place before rehearsal officially got underway, he started conversing with a lady cello player seated beside him. Appearing to be about forty, she introduced herself as Jacqueline. Discussing their love of the instrument from an early age, she told Christian that when she began taking lessons in her early teens back home in Connecticut, she had a wonderful teacher named Mason Harrington.

Trying to hide his shock and showing no emotion, Christian said simply "I actually think I've heard of him."

In the second week of September, Christian received a phone call from the Providence County District Attorney's office's secretary to ask if he could come in to meet with the D.A. in a few days. He agreed to the meeting and went to work on reviewing everything to be well prepared.

He drove to Providence on that beautiful late summer day and parked at a lot about a half mile away from the D.A.'s office. Walking along, he marveled at the beauty of the extremely well-maintained historic area of the city that featured many Colonial-style homes from the 18th and 19th centuries, as well as museums, and art galleries. It truly appealed to the old soul in him, and with a few minutes to spare he sat on a bench to appreciate the view. He closed his eyes for a few moments, and when he opened them, he appeared to be in Revolutionary War times, with horse drawn carriages rolling up the dirt roads and people dressed in the clothing of that period. Two men coming from opposite directions approached each other about twenty feet in front of him. As they shook hands, he could hear one say to the other, "I've been looking forward to our meeting Mr. Van Buren." Suddenly, his vision was interrupted by a large city bus stopping near him to let off passengers.

He could only assume that he had just had a brush with an ancestor of long ago.

After waiting a bit, he was finally called in to speak with D.A. Grasso. He said upon their meeting, "I've heard many good things about you. You seem to be quite an amazing individual and I love the idea that you could help us with criminal investigations."

Christian responded, "It's been emphasized to me that I should use my gifts wisely."

The D.A. replied, "You're a special young man."

He continued, "Now I want you to know that we have followed up on the information you've provided. I'm happy to report positive findings. With the assistance of the registry of motor vehicles archives, we were able to determine the owner of the automobile during that span." He then added, "and it may not surprise you to learn that he was a man with a criminal history who was known to the police." Christian replied, "Well no, that doesn't seem like a total surprise."

D.A. Grasso then dropped the most significant finding of all.

"And we sent a work crew to excavate the location that you provided, and sure enough, skeletal remains were found. With dental records, the forensic pathologists were able to determine that the victim was in fact the man you suspected."

Christian looked down at the floor in silence. All at once he was both awed and humbled by the powers he possessed. He finally looked up and asked the D.A., "Does the man's family know?"

Grasso responded, "Yes, we informed them two days ago." Christian then asked, "Do they know how you were able to locate him?"

The D.A. said, "We simply told them that we acted on an anonymous tip. I don't think it would be good to involve you or your methods."

"Yes, it's better that way," agreed Christian.

The D.A. then sat on the edge of his desk, crossed his arms, and had a bit of a frown on his face. He began "Now... here's the downside of it all. The governor had the power to commute Pinto's sentence, and I believe he did the right thing. He doesn't however have the power to declare Shane Tourino's killer guilty and shuffle him off to prison."

"I do understand," Christian replied, "that this is a different type of situation."

"Yes," said the D.A., "This is going to require enough solid proof that a grand jury will be convinced enough for us to get an indictment, and then of course, a guilty verdict at a trial." He concluded "With all due respect, your visions aren't going to be enough to convince a jury, and I can see the defense attorney having a field day with it."

"I'd like to make a request sir, and I'm not sure how realistic it is, but I hope you'll consider I,t" Christian asked. "Now that this case appears to have been re-opened, would you allow me to work on some kind of basis with the investigators who are involved? I told D.A. O'Malley that many psychics and mediums have worked with law enforcement agencies to solve many crimes, and I think I've already demonstrated that potential."

"It is hard to dispute what you say Christian, and although it's a bit unorthodox, it certainly has a well-established precedent," the D.A. responded.

Christian added, "The more I know about names and details, the better the chance I night have other visions that help provide clues that help lead to solving this."

D.A. Grasso then started to wrap up the meeting by saying, "Okay Christian... let me run this by the police commissioner and I will get back to you as soon as possible."

He left feeling optimistic that their desire to finally solve the crime would prompt them to accept any help he could provide.

32

ONE EVENING IN mid-September, Christian received a phone call from Dennis Collier who stated that he was a friend and co-author of the psychic Lilly Larsson he had met a few weeks prior. Christian told him that he had discussed with Willy the idea of him working on a biography with a writer and found that he was open to the idea. He told Christian at the time, "If your vision showed you that it's going to happen... then I have to go with that."

They arranged for the three of them to meet up that weekend.

The trio got together at Willy's tiny apartment that Sunday afternoon and they all hit it off well. Dennis was fascinated with Willy's story and very enthused about its potential. Willy said to Dennis, "I owe everything to young Christian here. He was a gift sent from God. If it weren't for him, I'd still be wasting away in prison."

Dennis replied "I don't think I could sit down and make

up a better story. It has that element of the supernatural that really puts a different spin on it.... but it's real life, not science fiction."

He continued, "I even think it would have the potential to be made into a movie. I'm quite confident some Hollywood producer would be very intrigued with the idea."

Added Christian, "As I told Willy, I had a vision of him speaking from a lectern to a large crowd holding up a book. There are personal appearances involving this project in his future."

"Well," replied Dennis, "I could definitely see him going on television and radio shows to promote a book like this. It also seems like a great topic for motivational speaking. He will rise from some of the lowest of lows to some pretty good success."

"I definitely think people are attracted to that kind of story," said Christian.

"And I'll tell you another thing Christian," said Dennis, "when we're done with this, I wonder if you'd consider agreeing to work with me on your biography. That would be an absolute winner as well."

Christian paused... shook his head slightly, and said, "I'm really going to have to give that a lot of thought. But I will say that I really wouldn't look forward to the attention and notoriety my story would bring."

Willy and Dennis agreed to meet twice a week to start work on the project.

When Christian arrived home, his mother came in his room to tell him that her mother called her with some concerning news. Emily's father Dan had been having some physical issues recently and is scheduled to undergo a test to determine if he has pancreatic cancer. Emily was trying to maintain a positive outlook, but knew that if that were the diagnosis, his chances of long-term survival were very slim. Christian had a very brief vision that did not show a good outcome but kept it to himself.

He felt an overwhelming sense of sadness thinking about the fact that his dear grandfather had to deal for nearly two decades with the knowledge that he caused the death of a young man and now very likely had to face his own.

33

CHRISTIAN ACHIEVED A career milestone at his father's auto dealership that week in one of his capacities as a salesman. He managed to sell a pristine 1998 silver Lamborghini Diablo to a gentleman who owned a high-end nightclub in Providence. Bryan was very impressed at how he handled the transaction from beginning to end. Christian's impeccably tailored, high-quality suit and high level of maturity allowed him to be taken seriously well beyond his eighteen-and-a-half years.

That week he received a phone call from Donald Henderson, a detective with the Providence Police. He asked Christian to come to police headquarters the following morning at 9 a.m. He was optimistic that this was a sign of their willingness to allow him to assist in the investigation in any way he could.

He arrived at the Washington Street station promptly and was escorted to Lt. Henderson's office. He would tell Christian that he had never utilized these types of methods before and tended to be skeptical, but that his colleagues told him how impressed they had been so far. The idea of cracking a case that had gone cold so many years before prompted him to be open to almost anything. The detective did stress the need for complete confidentiality and required Christian to sign a non-disclosure agreement and that he should only report directly to him. Christian signed the form and assured Detective Henderson that he would honor it and keep it just between them.

Driving home, Christian started to feel a bit of the pressure of expectation and hoped that his powers would not fail him in this case. It was not always something he could simply turn on when needed, though he did find that intense concentration could at times be a precursor. This could be a real test and might prove to be quite a challenge.

Arriving home, he found his mother and sister in tears, as they had received news that confirmed their worst fears. The test on his grandfather Dan did in fact reveal pancreatic cancer. The doctor determined that it was fairly advanced and did not give an optimistic prognosis. Christian tried his best to comfort them and keep hope alive, even though his vision indicated otherwise. He pledged to himself not to reveal any of what he saw.

He spent that evening reflecting on his grandfather and all the good memories they had together over the years. But there now were two distinctly different aspects when thinking about him. There was the wonderful, happy-go-lucky doting grandpa that he had been throughout Christian's whole life, and there was the man who was responsible for his father's death. It seemed almost impossible to think of one side without those thoughts conflicting with the other. He was hoping that maybe some time before his grandfather passed, he might be able to help him be at peace and seek forgiveness for that one horribly tragic incident.

Christian would have to give a lot of thought to how to approach such a sensitive topic.

34

THE FOLLOWING EVENING, nearing time to go to bed, he decided to focus very intensely to attempt to call up some vision that would provide more clues that would help in the investigation.

After pondering what avenue to take, he thought that attempting to connect with the victim might be the best route with which to start. He closed his eyes and very slowly started to softly whisper his name over and over... "Shane Tourino... Shane Tourino. He tried to focus on the memory he had of the one photo he had seen in the newspaper article from the time he was reported missing. After a few minutes, he started to weave other words and phrases into his chants. "Shane... they killed you... they put you in the trunk of a car... they buried your body... Shane.... tell me who did it.

Christian was suddenly staring down a dark, long, narrow tunnel. He could see what appeared to be the figure of a person standing at the far end, and focusing on it, the figure seemed to be walking very slowly toward him. He could hear the faint sound of footsteps echoing, and very gradually they became louder and louder. Finally coming into view, he could see it was a man dressed in a black suit with a white shirt and black tie, and as he stopped about ten feet away, he recognized the face as that of Shane.

Wanting to act quickly before he disappeared, Christian asked, "Shane... can you tell me who did this to you?"

There was a long pause and Shane finally said, "You need to find Domenic Barbaro... he was there and can tell you all about it." He then turned slowly and started to walk back down the tunnel until he was out of sight. The vision then slowly faded and Christian was lying in bed pondering what he just saw. He quickly got up and wrote down the name Domenic Barbaro and now felt he could call Detective Henderson with this piece of information.

He called police headquarters the following morning and supplied the name that was revealed to him in his vision. Detective Henderson assured him that he would research the person to determine if there was any connection between him and the man who owned the BMW at the time of the murder.

Henderson called back late that afternoon and had very interesting information to reveal. Domenic Barbaro was known to Providence Police and had a few arrests, most recently one in 2022. This most recent charge was racketeering, which resulted in a five-year sentence which he was currently serving at the same prison from which Willy had been recently released. An important bit of information known to police was that he was part of an organized crime syndicate that also included Ralph Morgana, the man who owned the BMW in the period in question.

Henderson now felt that he had an individual that he could question about the murder, though he didn't expect Barbaro to co-operate, at least not initially. He was going to have to be resourceful and use every tactic at his disposal to create an incentive for him to provide enough information to implicate Morgana. When he felt he had done his due diligence, he would be paying a visit to the Adult Correctional Institution to conduct a preliminary interview with Barbaro.

After consulting with the police commissioner and the county district attorney, Henderson was set to conduct the interrogation by going to the prison to meet with Barbaro. Correction Officers escorted the inmate, dressed in a gray jumpsuit, to a small office, as Henderson entered a moment later. After stating his name and his position, Henderson stated, "As you well know, Shane Tourino was murdered in March of 2018. In fact, someone with close ties to the incident has revealed that you were involved. So why don't you level with me and tell me exactly what happened?"

Barbaro got defensive and said, "I would like to have an attorney present if you're going to ask me these kinds of question."

Replied Henderson, "This is just an informal conversation and we are under no obligation to supply you with an attorney. Tell me what you know."

"Look," said Barbaro, "I'm set to wrap up in a year and a half. I've made the decision to leave this gang business behind. I'm going to move out to Iowa near my sister. Her husband owns a business and he's going to give me a job." He concluded, "I've had it with this garbage life."

"So, you must remember the details of Tourino's murder," said Henderson. "You don't forget something like that."

"Look," snapped Barbaro, "I did not kill the guy... and there's no proof that I did."

"Well," replied Henderson, "the D.A. wants to finally resolve this, and he's looking for a scalp. Right now, yours is the best we have. Being an accessory is a serious charge." Barbaro sat silent for several moments and Henderson got up from his seat and said, "Your Iowa plans may be put off for quite a while. Think about it." He then got to the doorway and motioned for the correction officers to return him to his block.

Henderson would bide his time and also had one more approach up his sleeve.

35

CHRISTIAN DECIDED TO pay a visit to his grandfather in the days following the devastating news he had received. That Saturday morning, they sat on his back porch as Christian tried to reassure him not to lose hope and that there were treatment options available. Though he was quite certain of the sad outcome, he tried hard to put on a brave, optimistic front. His grandfather pretty clearly did not share the view and seemed resigned to his fate. He said, "I have to be realistic. What are the chances that I'm going to be one of the very small percentage of patients that survives this... especially with it being this advanced?"

"Grandpa," said Christian, "Let's just take it a day at a time, and know that we'll all be here for you."

Christian then pivoted to another topic, saying "You know Grandpa... I know that thing you and I talked about a while back has been haunting you for nearly twenty years. I want to tell you something else about it." He went on to tell him how several weeks prior he visited Andrew's gravesite and coincidentally encountered his sister there. He went on to relay the entire story about telling her about being struck by lightning and the powers that it left him with, and how it led to him learning the truth. Christian emphasized to his grandfather that he did not mention his role in Andrew's death.

"So how did she accept that whole story?" asked Dan.

"Well," answered Christian, "I was able to supply her with some info that completely convinced her. She was very receptive to it all, and we left on very good terms. She later sent me a photo of Andrew."

Christian continued, "So what I was thinking Grandpa, is that maybe I could arrange a meeting with you, me and her, and you could explain exactly what happened and ask for her forgiveness. I think it would take a tremendous amount of weight off your shoulders and allow you to make peace with the whole situation. Would you think about it?"

Dan looked down, deep in thought for a moment, and finally looked up and said "Well... there really isn't much they can do to me now I suppose. I still would prefer that it didn't become public knowledge. It would create such a dark cloud over my whole life, it would be the main thing I'd be remembered for." He then said, "If you think we can just keep it between you, me, and her, I'd be open to it."

Christian told him that when she sent him Andrew's photo, she included her phone number, and that he would call her to see if she would be interested in meeting someone who could provide the final chapter of that terrible incident nineteen years prior.

He called Melanie later that day and she agreed to meet in the parking lot of St. Columba's Chapel in Middletown at two o'clock.

At the agreed upon time they met, Christian introduced his grandfather to Melanie, and they sat on a bench to proceed. He started off by telling her that the first time they spoke, and he told her the story, he left out one important detail, but that she would soon understand why. It was Dan's turn to speak.

He took a deep breath and looked Melanie in the eyes with a very somber look on his face and began, "I have a major confession to make to you and your parents. I am the person who is responsible for your brother's death." Speechless, she had a stunned look on her face as he slowly continued. "He had gotten my daughter Emily pregnant, and I confronted him and insisted that he marry her. When he showed no interest in that, I lost control and hit him. After the second punch he went down hard."

He added, "I just panicked... I didn't know what to do... so I left."

Dan continued, "When I found out the next morning that he died, I was horrified. But I saw they arrested some guy who seemed like a real criminal type... and I guess I just didn't have the courage to come forward. It has haunted me every day since."

Melanie turned to Christian and said, "I guess I can see why you left out part of the story."

Christian added, "And as my grandfather told me when I first approached him about what my gift allowed me to discover, my grandmother had already become disabled at that time, and he was her sole caretaker. He kept quiet because if he ended up going to jail, he didn't know how she would get by."

Dan interjected, "I am very proud of my grandson for his successful efforts in getting that poor man released from prison. I could never possibly make that up to the guy."

He turned to Melanie and said, "I hope you will accept my sincere apology, but I do completely understand if you don't. In the meantime, I'd like to go inside the chapel and pray."

When Dan went inside, Christian told her that his grandfather had very recently been diagnosed with what was very likely a fatal form of cancer, and almost certainly did not have much time left.

She thanked him and departed.

Christian walked into the chapel to find Dan just finishing up his prayers. As they walked out together, Dan said, "I hope God will have mercy on my soul."

Three weeks later he would find out.

36

DETECTIVE HENDERSON HAD a meeting with the police commissioner and the commissioner of the department of corrections and was ready with a new strategy to approach inmate Barbaro. He had also received access to his family contact information in the prison's files and found contact information listed for Barbaro's sister in Iowa. He placed a call to her to confirm what Barbaro had told him about his plan to move out there and work for her husband upon his release. She was able to verify that this was in fact the plan. Henderson then made his second trip to the correctional facility to interview Barbaro once more to attempt to make progress on the case.

Once face to face with Barbaro, he started, "I may have an interesting proposal for you, but I'd really like to hear your version of the events as they happened. Just tell me what you saw."

He responded, "I need to know that I'm going to be

protected in some way. I can't go naming names and expect to survive here for too long."

"Okay," said Henderson, "here's what I can tell you. If you testify in court about who did the actual killing, the governor has agreed to immediately transfer you to a facility in Iowa near where your sister lives. If we go on to get a guilty verdict, he will shave one year off your sentence, and you'll be free to start working with your brother-in-law and start a new life out there."

Barbaro then said, "Give me a couple minutes to think about this," and he put his head in his hands.

He finally looked up and said "Okay... I'm ready... but on a couple of conditions. You can't record anything I say today, and I want you to get an agreement in writing from the governor before I actually testify."

Henderson responded, "No recording, and I'm pretty sure I can get that in writing." He was also relieved, knowing that he didn't have another actual witness to the killing and that Barbaro didn't call his bluff.

"Okay," said Barbaro, "so a group of us were at Ralph Morgana's house in Cranston. He was renting a house that didn't have any neighbors nearby, and there was a big backyard leading out to the woods. He had it all planned." He then stopped and said, "I should back up a bit and tell you that he found out that Shane Tourino had a brother-in-law who was an F.B.I. agent. Someone saw Tourino talking to him in a restaurant in Providence, and Morgana was convinced he was an informant. He had to go."

Barbaro continued. "So, Morgana lured him way out back

and shot him in the back of the head. I saw the whole thing from less than a hundred feet away." There was a long pause as Barbaro seemed to stare straight ahead, contemplating the grim memory.

"So then," he finally resumed, "Morgana ordered me to go dig a hole at a very specific out of the way location right under the Route 95 expressway in Providence. He handed me a shovel and told me to call him when it was ready. Just as I was about to leave, I could see them wrapping the body in a big brown tarp and lifting it into the trunk of Morgana's BMW. When I got back to the house later after digging the hole, I was told that he and Norby Gioso had taken the body there."

Barbaro then indicated that he never heard any reference to the incident again by anyone who was present, and that from then on, it almost seemed like an unspoken rule that you don't get on Morgana's bad side.

Henderson then informed the inmate that if everything moves forward and that they can get an indictment, he may be asked to meet with the prosecution's attorneys about testifying. Barbaro's main focus now would be to do what he had to do to get an early release from prison and start new.

37

THE FUNERAL FOR his grandfather was held in early October, and that night, Christian had a difficult time getting to sleep. He couldn't stop thinking what the other side was like for him now that he crossed over. Was it the beautiful, miraculous experience so full of love that so many who've had a glimpse of it describe? Or, did that one major transgression cause something less pleasant?

Almost on cue, he saw a shimmering image in the corner of his room that seemed to take far longer to become clear than all the previous images he had experienced. Looking more like Christian's earliest memories of him, it was Grandpa Dan standing there with a wonderful, loving smile. He finally started to speak.

"My boy... only you could do it... you lifted a terrible burden off my back... and you made my crossing over as beautiful as it could be."

Christian was sobbing as his grandfather slowly faded into the wall.

A few days later, he got another piece of sad news. He received an official looking letter from an attorney in Connecticut informing him that Mason's brother Charles had passed away suddenly about a week before. It explained that Charles had recently added Christian to his will, and that he had an inheritance coming to him. The letter included a check for $25,000, and he would also be receiving Mason's 1978 Mercedes-Benz and his bag of golf clubs. There was a telephone number to call in order to arrange pick up for what was left to him.

Christian called the number and spoke to one of Charles' nephews. They agreed to meet the following Sunday at the house Christian had previously visited in Greenwich so that he could pick up the items. He drove the flatbed tow truck from his father's dealership and loaded the Mercedes onboard. The nephew told Christian that his uncle told him the whole story and was eternally grateful for having met him.

Christian decided he would play one full round of golf with Mason's clubs to further share their connection. He would display the classic Mercedes in the showroom of his father's dealership as a wonderful example of the type of vehicles they feature, however, with a *Not for Sale* sign affixed.

As for the money left to him, he very much wanted to do something positive and charitable. That would require a lot of careful consideration.

The idea finally came to him that he would create a scholarship in Mason's name that would be given each year to a high school graduate who was going on to attend a music college. It would seem fitting to limit it to a school or schools in Mason's hometown area of Greenwich. He thought it should also be limited to only public schools, as those students were more likely in need of financial help for college than private school students. The concept was falling into place quickly. It would be named *The Mason Harrington Music Scholarship*, and $2,000 per year would be granted to the student Christian selected to be the most deserving. He would soon contact that city's school district to turn the idea into reality.

He ultimately contacted the head guidance counselors of three high schools, and they established guidelines for how it would operate. Interested students would fill out an application provided by their school and write an accompanying letter explaining why they felt they deserved the scholarship. Christian would receive them all by March 15th and would review them all and select the one recipient. He was very much looking forward to the process.

38

BY LATE OCTOBER, Christian was notified by Providence County D.A. Grasso that Morgana was indicted and that a trial was scheduled to begin on January 10th. He asked Christian about the possibility of testifying, and while the D.A. said that type of testimony was very unorthodox, it was not entirely unprecedented. Christian expressed to him that he would really prefer not to, and very much wanted to avoid the kind of attention that would likely bring. The D.A. told him that they could state at the trial that an anonymous tip had led them to where Tourino was buried, and that Barbaro was questioned due to being one of the few associates of Morgana's left whose whereabouts was known. Christian was anxious to watch the progress of the trial when it did start, planning to keep a close eye on the news updates daily.

That month, a premonition he had his first day home from the hospital would transpire. One morning a man walked into the showroom whom he recognized as actor James Fiorentini and expressed interest in the white Ferrari on the lot. Knowing from his vision that he would ultimately buy it, Christian stepped right up to help him and knew there would be a fairly generous commission on this sale. A little while later he said to his father, "You know, we've been talking about putting together another local cable TV commercial. Remember what I told you the day I came home.... this is our man." Bryan couldn't help but laugh and shake his head. Although he had just turned nineteen, Christian was establishing himself as a competent salesman.

Willy had also become a valued member of the team at the dealership. He had his driver's license again after nearly twenty years and was able to drive to pick up auto parts the mechanics needed. On occasion, was able to do brief test drives of very expensive European cars that he could have only dreamed of driving earlier in his life. He had even started dating the sister of one of the secretaries and was establishing a solid, productive, life for himself. Willy also continued to work on his life story with his co-author Dennis Collier and reported that they were making tremendous progress. He said that there was interest from the company that published Dennis's previous book, and that if all went according to plan, this book could be available by the summertime. Christian often marveled at Willy's ability and desire to make up for lost time in such a productive way and sometimes referred to him as "Our American Success Story."

Christian would attend another get-together with his medium/psychic friends the following Sunday afternoon. He updated them with many of his recent experiences, and they shared some of theirs as well. It was the one social situation he engaged in where he felt completely comfortable, as opposed to his usual slight alienation. One of them encouraged him to start doing one-on-one session at The Other Side Café, saying that it could be financially lucrative enough to possibly earn a living. He wanted to remind them that when he experienced his first visits from his biological father, he was told to use his gifts wisely. Christian wanted to make it clear to the rest that he did not want to appear the least bit judgmental, but that he wasn't sure he would feel comfortable profiting from his gifts.

He also shared a very recent story that presented a real dilemma and a great deal of sadness for him. At Thanksgiving dinner at his aunt's house, he saw his twenty-four-year-old cousin Jared who was home visiting from New York City.

Jared was an extremely intelligent young man who had graduated from Yale University two years prior. He was now working on Wall Street in a very high-paying position in the financial industry and had also made a few very shrewd stock purchases that he was confident would make him wealthy. He told stories about having brushes with very well-known people, and his future looked incredibly bright. He was telling Christian that his plan was to work very hard and live a very basic, modest lifestyle and retire hopefully before he was forty with ten million dollars in the bank. At that point he would then travel to exotic and interesting locations all over the world, work on his "bucket list," and live a life of ease and privilege. Christian was listening intently, and just as Jared got up to go get a piece of pie in the kitchen, a vision began to materialize.

Jared was lying in a hospital bed all hooked up to tubes, appearing to be maybe ten years older than he was now. Several family members were standing at his bedside, and he then saw a few of them start to hug each other, crying.

When Jared returned with his piece of pie, Christian desperately wanted to tell him that maybe he should start to enjoy some of these plans while he was young in his twenties and thirties, and to not let these prime years pass by. He knew, however, that Jared knew of his gifts and would immediately assume that he had foreseen something terrible about his future. Christian was terribly torn but simply didn't know how to suggest anything without arousing suspicion.

After telling his friends the story, they all agreed that this was a terrible position for a psychic to be in, and that they probably would have kept it to themselves as well.

Christian concluded, "This is the one aspect of this gift that I absolutely hate, and sometimes I feel like I would give it up in a minute if I could."

39

EARLY JANUARY ROLLED around, and Ralph Morgana's trial was set to begin. The prosecution had met with Barbaro and went over all the questions they would ask at trial, as well as possible questions the defense attorney might ask. Though he was really the only true witness available to the murder, they felt his version was strong enough to convince a jury of Morgana's guilt.

As the trial began, Barbaro was not present in the courtroom but was being held in a holding cell in the basement of the courthouse until he was needed to testify. Morgana sat expressionless at the defense attorney's table. After the opening statements, one of the first witnesses that was called was the Providence County forensic examiner who had studied Tourino's skeletal remains. He testified that the only visible wounds relating to the murder were what appeared to be a bullet entry hole in the back of the skull, and an exit hole in the front.

The prosecution then had the detective in charge of the exhumation of Tourino's body testify. They brought out a large, illustrated map of the area showing Route 95 and several landmarks in the immediate vicinity, and had him point to the exact area where the body was found and mark it with a red marker. He also testified that the body was found wrapped tightly in a brown tarp.

They then had an employee of the Rhode Island Registry of Motor Vehicles testify that records showed that Morgana owned a black 2017 BMW sedan at the time Tourino was reported missing. After that it would be Barbaro's turn on the witness stand.

He was escorted into the courtroom by two court officers, as he shuffled along wearing leg irons and handcuffed in waist chains as was required of inmates from correctional facilities attending court. Barbaro took his place on the witness stand and was sworn in, then sat down. He glanced out at the courtroom and saw Morgana glaring at him and decided from that point he would not look anywhere near his direction.

The prosecution then began with a series of questions that allowed Barbaro to explain how they became associated several years back, the various illegal activities in which they engaged, and Morgana's strong suspicion that Tourino was an F.B.I. informant. The attorney then focused on the events that occurred on the day of the murder.

Barbaro was able to describe it all in detail just as he had to Henderson in their last meeting. His answers all seemed to validate what had been testified to by previous witnesses. He described the shots to the back of the head that would corroborate the pathologist's' finding of an entry wound in the back of the skull and an exit wound in the front. He identified the black BMW vehicle that the registry employee stated was owned by Barbaro at the time in question. He was shown a duplicate map of the area where the body had been exhumed that was not marked with the location and was able to mark the area where he dug the hole. The two maps were then shown to the jury to see that they matched. He described the body being wrapped in a brown tarp before it was loaded into Morgana's trunk. He answered the question about what occurred when he returned to the house after digging the hole, and that Morgana and Gioso had left to dispose of the body.

The defense attempted a cross examination but were unable to cast any serious doubt on his testimony.

Court adjourned for the day, and for security purposes, Barbaro was transferred to a county house of correction a half hour away in New Bedford, Massachusetts and placed in protective custody. The concern was that there could be a leak about Barbaro's testimony and that Morgana might contact inmates at the facility who could make an attempt on his life. Barbaro had to remain in the area in case he was called back to the witness stand.

The trial dragged on for a couple more days, and finally closing arguments were delivered. The jury deliberated and only took two hours to reach a verdict. Morgana was found guilty of first-degree murder and ultimately sentenced to life in prison.

Christian had been following reports of the trial daily and was pleased that his powers allowed for the man responsible for Shane Tourino's death to receive his due punishment, regardless of how belated. Barbaro was then transferred to a medium-security prison in Iowa, within an hour from where his sister lived. As promised by the Rhode Island authorities, his sentence was ultimately commuted one year early, and he was released to the custody of his sister and her husband on the condition that he would be employed by him. Domenic Barbaro would live the remainder of his life there and manage to avoid any further trouble.

40

CHRISTIAN CONTACTED THREE high schools in Greenwich that agreed to offer the opportunity of being awarded the Mason Harrington Music Scholarship to the upcoming graduating class. By late March, he began receiving large packets from each school containing the applications from hopeful students, each accompanied by a letter making their case for why they deserved the scholarship.

He greatly enjoyed reading the letters from students who were only roughly a year younger than himself. He was very impressed and could completely relate to their passion and desire to embark on a career in music, with a wide range of genres represented, from jazz to classical to mainstream rock and pop. One applicant he thought must be some type of an old soul like himself. He was a clarinet player who wanted to influence a revival of the old big band era from the 1940s and early 1950s.

Another applicant really captured his fascination above all

others. Her name was Rebecca Moore, and like him, she played the cello. She wrote of her tireless obsession with mastering the instrument and even mentioned a couple of classical pieces which were among Christian's favorites. One of her main goals in life was to become a member of a symphony orchestra. She had been accepted to attend the Berklee School of Music in Boston in the fall.

But one thing that really caught his attention was her inclusion of the fact that her grandfather had played in the high school band with Mason back in the 1960s and had been friendly with him. When she told her grandfather that she was applying for the Mason Harrington Music Scholarship, he remembered him very fondly, and said that it would be a true cosmic connection if she were to be the first recipient.

All of these factors combined virtually ensured that she would be Christian's selection.

It was in very early May that Greenwich High School would be holding its Senior Scholarship Night, and Christian would drive down to be on hand to present his award. He sought out and introduced himself to the school's head guidance counselor Heather Greene who had coordinated the scholarships and the event. She had informed Rebecca the day before that she would be receiving the award created by Christian. Heather scanned those milling about the lobby in front of the auditorium before the event began and spotted Rebecca, who was with her parents. She called her over and formally introduced her to Christian as the young man who made it happen.

When Christian and Rebecca's eyes met, there was an

instant attraction. Christian congratulated her on her application package and assured her that he knew she was the best choice almost instantly. They began speaking of their mutual love of the cello and their goals for success with it in the future. Christian, who tended to be a bit awkward with girls, had never felt as comfortable as he did at that moment. The chemistry between the two was palpable.

It was time for the event to begin, and people filed into the auditorium and took their seats. As part of the band, Rebecca took her place with the others in the area off to the right of the front of the stage. Christian was seated on the stage with all the others to present scholarships. After several were awarded, it was Christian's turn, and he was introduced by Ms. Greene and approached the lectern.

He informed the crowd that the Mason Harrington Music Scholarship was recently established in honor of a man who grew up in Greenwich and went on to considerable success as a cello player in a major symphony orchestra in New York City. He then continued, "The school administration allowed me to select the recipient of the scholarship, and in reviewing the applications, there were many impressive young musicians who certainly deserve help with their tuition to college to further their studies in music. One applicant almost immediately rose above the rest, and when I found out that her grandfather had played in the high school band with Mr. Harrington... It seemed almost too good to be true."

He let several seconds pass and finally announced, "The very first recipient of the Mason Harrington Music Scholarship is... Rebecca Moore"

The crowd cheered as she got up from her seat in the band section and walked up onto the stage. Christian desperately wanted to kiss her at that moment but controlled himself and simply shook her hand and handed her the award, with both of them smiling broadly. She then returned to her seat with the band, and he to his seat on the stage.

As other awards were presented, Christian and Rebecca looked at each other from afar and smiled. After a few moments, he began to lapse into a vision of a future event.

In it, he appeared to be in the very same auditorium, sitting out in the crowd, watching a similar event as to what had been taking place. Ms. Greene announced, "I'd now like to bring Rebecca Casey up to present the Mason Harrington Music Scholarship."

Rebecca walked up to the lectern and spoke into the microphone. "Five years ago, my husband Christian created this scholarship before I knew him, and I was extremely fortunate and blessed to be its first recipient. It was a tremendous honor. This year's scholarship goes to..." - and then the vision trailed off and faded.

It took Christian a minute or two to fully digest what he had just experienced, but it eventually became clear. This wonderful, magical, fateful meeting would ultimately result in his marriage to Rebecca.

At the conclusion of the event, he made sure to say goodbye and suggested that maybe they could get together to play a cello duet sometime soon. He drove home feeling like he was on a cloud.

41

WILLY AND DENNIS had worked hard all winter on his story, and the publishing company he had worked with previously showed great interest in the final manuscript. The pair had signed a contract in February for its publication. The book, entitled "My Miraculous Return from Hell" was scheduled to be released on June 1st. A publicist that Dennis worked with went to work scheduling appearances for them on local television and radio shows as well as book signings at various bookstores. Willy would be entering a whole new world, and both Dennis and Christian worked with him on public speaking and practiced asking him the kinds of questions that media types who interviewed them might ask.

In the book itself, they respected Christian's desire to be anonymous. Dennis gave him the name "Martin St. Laurent" for a slightly exotic image and referred to him as being originally from Montreal.

The first event they did as a promotion was very fittingly

held at "The Other Side" bookstore. It took place in a large back room that served as an all-purpose conference room where mediums would often hold their public events and readings. Though Christian was in attendance, no one there was made aware that he was the person described in the book.

As the event began, one of the managers got up to speak to roughly sixty people on hand about the newly released book and introduced both Dennis and Willy. Dennis was the first to get up to speak, recalling when he heard the story for the first time nine months prior, and feeling instantly that it was something that would appeal to many. He spoke of being in awe of meeting Willy for the first time, and how well-adjusted he was with a total lack of bitterness. Dennis complimented him for being so well-spoken and intelligent, and that working on this book was one of the more rewarding experiences of his career.

It was now time for Willy to speak.

As he was introduced and made his way up to the lectern, the applause was nearly deafening and became a standing ovation. Willy had never experienced anything like it and was practically moved to tears. He went on to explain how appreciative he was that the extremely unusual gifts of one young man who was relentless in trying to do the right thing helped to turn his life completely around. "It was like an angel was sent to me," he said. The audience was very moved by his eloquence, and by the end of the evening, thirty of the books were sold. Willy felt like a celebrity signing books for customers but remained completely humble.

It would be the first of numerous appearances, and by Christmas, roughly 40,000 copies of the book had sold worldwide. Dennis began to shop the story around to film producers to potentially bring the story to the screen.

Willy was able to move into a slightly larger, nicer apartment, and bought himself a sporty Alfa Romeo coupe from Bryan's dealership.

42

IT WAS A Sunday morning in mid-July when Christian met his three golf partners very early at a local course for their weekly foursome. He was gearing up for a tournament that would be held in Massachusetts in a couple of weeks, and he felt he was playing the best golf of his life. He was leading his mates in this particular round by several strokes and was standing on the fairway of the 8th hole waiting for his turn.

Without any warning, an errant golf ball from across the way struck Christian on the left temple and dropped him to the ground. His friends all came running over, and while he never did lose consciousness, he was stunned and disoriented. They got him to his feet, but seeing that he was not steady, they borrowed a golf cart from a nearby group and sat him in it, then drove him to the clubhouse. From there, one of his partners drove him to the hospital to be checked out.

After doing X-rays and a CT scan, it was discovered that he had a very slight fracture on the left side of his skull. His mother and father arrived shortly after, finding him lying on a gurney very near where he was fifteen months prior after being struck by lightning. This time they were very relieved to see that he was alert and speaking. The doctor made the decision to admit him for observation for a day or two.

His parents, along with sister Shannon, came back to visit that evening and brought him his favorite gourmet chocolates to enjoy. His sister said to him, "What is it with you and golf courses? Are you sure you shouldn't stop going to them?"

As they all laughed, Christian retorted "You'd have to cut off my right arm. On second thought, make it my leg so I could still play the cello."

A short while later, his new girlfriend Rebecca came into the room to visit. Later on, Emily began to tell her about what it was like the previous year when Christian was in a coma for a week, and how the family kept a constant vigil. She was very relieved to say, "It doesn't appear that's going to be necessary this time."

After spending two nights, the doctor decided that he was set to be discharged on Tuesday afternoon. Dr. Bergman, the physician from his first stay the previous year, stopped by his room to say hello and to see how he was doing. After a brief chat, Christian said to the doctor, "There's something really strange going on. It's been well over forty-eight hours since I was hit in the head by the ball... and I have not had one psychic or medium experience since. That is very unusual. These types of things would happen in some form virtually every day... sometimes several times a day. Do you think..."

Dr. Bergman thought for a moment and finally said, "What

occurred to you last year is unbelievably rare... and for another incident that reverses that effect, I believe would be even more rare. I'd be very surprised if I were able to find a similar case, but I will call Dr. Woodward and get his thoughts."

Could the blow to the head from being struck by a golf ball somehow undo the bizarre effect of the lightning strike from fifteen months prior? When he was lying in bed that night at home, he tried to focus hard and concentrate on his father Andrew to see if he could prompt a visit or a vision of some type. There was nothing, and after about a half hour he gave up trying. The following night he tried to contact Mason, and still nothing.

He began thinking back a few days to see if he could recall the very last paranormal experience he had. He finally remembered that it was the evening before being struck, sitting with Rebecca, there was a very brief vision. In it, she said to him, "I'm so glad you're happy about feeling normal again." He had no idea what that was a reference to at the time, but it was now clear.

He had mixed emotions about it all, as his acquired powers had created sort of a new identity for him. Although he had tried to keep his focus on those things he had always loved, it had added a whole new element to his life. He tried to recall all of the positive things that came from it—helping to solve two murders, getting two men released from prison—one who had become a dear friend, finding the truth about himself and where he came from, and meeting the wonderful young lady who was destined to be his wife. He was told early on by the man he discovered was his father to use his gift wisely, and he truly believed he had followed that advice.

He could now resume his life with some sense of normalcy. Perhaps now that he would have no fears of being asked to perform psychic or medium functions, he could call Dennis Collier about the possibility of working on that book he had suggested.

www.ingramcontent.com/pod-product-compliance
Lightning Source LLC
Chambersburg PA
CBHW070936250626
47159CB00009B/3274